"Want to shake on it?" he said, then held his hand out to her.

Hannah couldn't help but feel that she was falling in with his wishes a little too easily. But this was a deal that put the two of them on equal standing. And it was a good thing, too.

"I think we can make it work." She stretched her hand out and felt the warmth of his fingers as they slid through hers, then folded around her hand. Their palms sealed the agreement, but still her hand lingered inside of his a moment longer than necessary. Pulling back her hand, she slid it against her jean-clad thigh to ease the disturbing tingle from William's touch. How had a simple sign of an agreement turned into such an intimate touch? This new William, the relaxed, more easygoing William, seemed dangerous. She started to tell him that she had changed her mind, that this might not be a good idea, but how could she do that without admitting how much his touch had affected her?

Dear Reader,

When I finished my last book, *Sarah and the Single Dad*, I felt that the story wasn't over. I couldn't help but wonder what happened to Hannah and Lindsey after Lindsey received her heart donation. Hannah's a single mother with no family support, and I admired that not only had she always been there for her daughter, but she had been working in the background to get her nursing license so she could give them both a better life. It wasn't until I got to know Hannah better that I realized that she had always had a desire to work in the medical field. While the birth of her daughter had made some changes to her plans, I found her courage and tenacity inspiring and I hope you will, too.

Best wishes,

Deanne

THE NEUROSURGEON'S UNEXPECTED FAMILY

DEANNE ANDERS

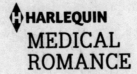

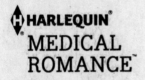

HARLEQUIN®
MEDICAL ROMANCE™

Recycling programs
for this product may
not exist in your area.

ISBN-13: 978-1-335-40449-7

The Neurosurgeon's Unexpected Family

Copyright © 2021 by Denise Chavers

This edition published by arrangement with Harlequin Books S.A.

For questions and comments about the quality of this book, please contact us at CustomerService@Harlequin.com.

Harlequin Enterprises ULC
22 Adelaide St. West, 40th Floor
Toronto, Ontario M5H 4E3, Canada
www.Harlequin.com

Printed in U.S.A.

Deanne Anders was reading romance while her friends were still reading Nancy Drew, and she knew she'd hit the jackpot when she found a shelf of Harlequin Presents in her local library. Years later she discovered the fun of writing her own. Deanne lives in Florida with her husband and their spoiled Pomeranian. During the day she works as a nursing supervisor. With her love of everything medical and romance, writing for Harlequin Medical Romance is a dream come true.

Books by Deanne Anders

Harlequin Medical Romance

From Midwife to Mommy
The Surgeon's Baby Bombshell
Stolen Kiss with the Single Mom
Sarah and the Single Dad

Visit the Author Profile page at Harlequin.com.

To Barry. While you never could handle the dirty diapers, you handled all the bloody noses and broken bones much better than me. Together, we made a great team.

CHAPTER ONE

HANNAH REEVES SPOTTED the man she wanted the moment she stepped out of her patient's room. Standing not five feet from her, Dr. William Cooper's tall frame was propped against the wall. The neurosurgery department's Ice Prince was on duty today, which meant her patient, Mrs. Nabors, would be in the best of hands.

Only, this wasn't the same doctor whose frosty control had made him a legend in the operating room. His pale blue eyes were ringed with dark shadows and his mouth was drawn into a tired line, so she knew something was wrong. Was this about Mrs. Nabors's CT? Hannah had known the news wouldn't be good given the look the CT tech had sent her when they'd transferred the woman back to her bed.

"Shelley, I'm sorry. It's an emergency." He ran his hand through his thick brown hair, causing it to stick out in all directions. "I know… I'll make some calls. Just give me a few minutes, okay?"

Hannah was about to interrupt him when he finally ended the call. Trying not to look like she had been eavesdropping, she stepped closer and found herself even more worried about the man when she noted his wrinkled shirt and lab jacket. And what was that stain on his shirt? Something was definitely wrong here, but whatever it was, it would have to wait until her patient was taken care of.

"Did you get the radiology report on Mrs. Nabors's CT?" Hannah asked, hoping to get both her and the doctor's mind back on what was really important. While she had assured her patient's daughter that her mother would be okay, the older woman's recent onset of confusion and the CT techs reaction had Hannah worried.

"I spoke with the radiologist before I came up. Her stroke has converted to a bleed, as you suspected. I'll have to take her to the OR. I'm going to go talk to her family now. Can you ready her consent?" he asked.

"Sure, I'll be right back." Hannah headed to the unit coordinator's desk to retrieve the proper form. Fifteen minutes later, she watched as the orderlies transported Mrs. Nabors to the OR.

Finally, she could start her end-of-shift notes. She'd already finished her patient rounds, but wanted to double-check the chart records to make sure there weren't any new orders to pass on when she reported to the incoming night shift.

For a few minutes, she let herself relax in the cushioned office chair as she reviewed her patients' charts. Her feet had been screaming for mercy for the last hour, so she kicked her shoes off under the computer table and wiggled her toes. She stifled a moan of pleasure. Satisfied with her charting, she closed her files. Just another half hour and she would be done.

Her mind began to tick off all the things that had to be done tonight. There was dinner to cook, Lindsey's homework to check, and then her own schoolwork to do—lately it had turned into a contest between them to see who had the most homework each night. And then there was yesterday's email from her college instructor reminding her that she still hadn't lined up a preceptor for this semester. Had she taken on too much?

At least the dreaded history project had been completed the night before. The memory of Lindsey carrying in her papier-mâché model of the Alamo this morning brought tears to Hannah's eyes. She'd come so close to losing her... She said a silent prayer for Lindsey's heart donor family, then mentally added the cardiologist's appointment to her list of things to do this week.

Hannah looked back at the clock. She had just enough time to make one quick round on her patients before the night nurse arrived and took over. Apologizing to her poor feet, she forced them back into her shoes, promising a long rest as soon as her life slowed down.

"Yes, I understand it's late, but if you could possibly find someone... She's just a baby, she can't be that much trouble... But I'll pay double...triple? I know it's last minute. That's how emergency surgery works. It's not scheduled... No, I'm not trying to be rude... Okay, I understand. Can you at least tell me if you've had any luck finding someone full-time for the position…? Sure. I'll call back tomorrow during office hours. Thank you."

Hannah paused at the entrance to the doctor's lounge where her favorite neurosurgeon now sat. Had she heard him right? A baby?

Coupled with the few hints from the side of the conversation she'd heard earlier, she now had a good idea of what had upset the doctor. Hadn't she found herself panicking over the same thing many times before? Only, it didn't make sense that the single doctor would be having issues with childcare. She knew for a fact the man didn't have any children. If he had, he certainly would have mentioned them before now.

She thought of the big stack of books waiting for her at home. She should pretend she hadn't overheard his conversation and walk away, but she'd been there herself too many times.

"Hey, Dr. Cooper, we missed you at Marjorie's retirement party last night," Hannah said as she stepped into the room, grappling for a way to approach him about what she'd overheard. She really didn't want to appear to have been listening in on his conversation, but there wasn't really any way around it.

"That was last night?" he asked.

"The flyer's been on the door of the break-room for the last two weeks," she said. Marjorie had been one of his favorite nurses; it had been surprising when he hadn't showed up.

He leaned back in his chair and shook his head. He had the look of a man that had suddenly woken up and didn't quite know where he was. It was plain to see that he needed help.

"I'm sorry, Dr. Cooper, but I couldn't help overhear your conversation on the phone. Is there something I can do to help?" Hannah asked.

"You've dealt with all this childcare stuff with your daughter, Lindsey, right? Trying to find someone to watch her while you're working?" he asked.

"Sure, every parent has to at some point," she said. "Is there a problem?"

"Yes, I have a really big problem right now. I need someone to watch a baby for me. I thought the person I hired understood that I needed someone flexible with their hours. They're only temporary, but it was all I could arrange at the time. Now I've got Mrs. Nabors being prepped for surgery and I don't have anyone to take care of this baby. Do you know any childcare services that do after-hours?"

Hannah couldn't help but feel for the man. She'd had her own trials with child-minding while she'd been working and going to school, even though Lindsey had spent what seemed like half her life in the hospital before she'd received her transplant. Hannah remembered those days all too well, especially when she and Lindsey had first moved to Houston.

It was impossible for her not to offer to help him.

Don't do it! Getting involved in other people's lives is just asking for trouble, a voice deep inside her intoned.

As usual, Hannah ignored the declaration she recognized as her mother's—an ingrained voice from which she feared she'd never escape, no matter how hard she tried.

"Look, I've been where you are before. It sucks," she said. "There have been lots of times when I've had a friend save me by volunteering to watch Lindsey. Most of the time, they're single moms like me and I can repay the favor."

Maybe this is a mistake, but what else can I do? The man had to do the surgery and didn't need to be worried about anything before he opened up poor Mrs. Nabors's skull.

"I'd be glad to help," she told him. "It's almost shift change, and I have to go pick up Lindsey at her after-school program, but that's only five minutes away from here."

"Really, you wouldn't mind?" he asked.

Was her offer such a shock? Of course, he was a world-renowned neurosurgeon. He probably never found himself in the position of needing someone else's help.

"Like I said, I've been there. What's her name?" Hannah asked. When he looked at her blankly, she prompted, "The baby? Her name? Her age? The address where I need to go?"

His face froze for a second before it seemed his brain kicked in and took over. There was definitely something more than just a child-care issue bothering him.

"Her name is Avery. She's eleven months—no, I think she's still ten months. I'm honestly not sure. I should know that, shouldn't I?" he said, though Hannah wasn't sure if he was talking to her or to himself.

"I take it she's at your house?" she asked, tearing a sticky note from the pad closest to her and sliding it across to him as his phone rang.

Glancing up at her, he scribbled an address as he took the call. Picking up the sticky note, she recognized it as one of the more affluent areas of Houston.

"I'll be right there," he said to the caller before hitting the end button. "That was the OR. They're ready for me. Look, Hannah, I don't know how to tell you how much I appreciate this."

"It's not a problem, Dr. Cooper. Like I said earlier, I've been there. How long are you expecting to be in surgery?" she asked, thinking she'd need to make plans for supper if he was going to be late. She would have also liked to ask about the child's diet, whether she was still on baby food or eating table food, but Hannah knew he didn't have the time to answer all her questions. She'd just have to wait till she could question the babysitter.

"I shouldn't be too late. Hopefully no longer than two hours, but I won't know till I get in there and see the size of the bleed," he said as he stood to leave.

She saw the hesitation in his eyes. "Don't worry about Avery. I'll take good care of her. We'll be at your house whenever you get there," she said in the same calm tone she used with her patients when they were anxious.

"Okay. I'll be there as soon as possible," he said before exiting the lounge and heading down the hall to the elevator that would take him to the OR.

Hannah had always found the man to be a bit of a mystery and now she was even more curious about him. He had a ten-month-old baby girl staying at his house. Where was the child's mother? Was he the father? Maybe they were having some type of custody issue...

She heard that voice again telling her to mind her own business and stay out of other people's troubles, and this time she had to admit that it was good advice. But Hannah had been living her life her way for a long time now. She made her own decisions and helping out a coworker was the right thing to do.

"Wow!" Lindsey breathed as they pulled up to the large house clad in stone and dark wood. Two wrought-iron balconies jutted out from the second story, giving it the look of a long-ago castle.

"Yeah. Wow!" Hannah said as she parked at the front entrance.

As Lindsey raced to the front door, Hannah slowly climbed out of the car. The large yard, she noted, was manicured to perfection, azaleas bursting from their buds in pink and purple blooms and shrubs trimmed into precise angles. It was the perfect complement for the impressive mansion.

Hannah planned to buy her and Lindsey their own home as soon as her education was done and she had secured a permanent job with one of the neurosurgeons. But even in her wildest of dreams, she had known that a small suburban home on a postage-stamp-size yard was all she would ever be able to afford in the Houston real estate market.

Following her daughter up to the door, she ran a calming hand over Lindsey's hair as the girl hopped excitedly from foot to foot. The eleven-year old had spent so much of her life waiting for a heart transplant to allow her to experience everything other children took for granted, that now she seemed to race headlong into every situation—something Hannah herself had done today.

The heavy wood door and wrought-iron chandelier that hung above the front porch screamed money. Feeling like the country mouse that had come to town, Hannah rang the doorbell and waited.

"Who are you?" asked the girl who finally opened the door, giving the two of them the once-over.

This was Shelley? The girl couldn't be much older than eighteen.

"I'm Hannah and this is my daughter, Lindsey," she said as she moved closer to her daughter. "Dr. Cooper sent me to watch over Avery until he gets out of surgery."

"Hi, I'm Shelley. Are you Dr. Cooper's girlfriend or something?" The girl gave her another top-to-bottom look.

"No, just a friend and coworker," Hannah said, pointing to the hospital badge hanging from her scrub top.

"Well, I'm just glad someone showed up. I should have been out of here—" the girl pulled her phone from her back pocket "—thirty minutes ago. I'm going to be late for my study group. I tried to explain to Dr.

Cooper that I had to be there. College exams are coming up, you know?"

"Dr. Cooper had an emergent surgery or I'm sure he would have been here," Hannah said.

"Hey, I'm premed, so I get it. I thought we could make it work since it was only a temporary thing, you know, until he can get someone full time," the girl said, still standing in the open doorway. "He's a good guy and all that, so I really wanted to help him out."

"Can we come in please?" Hannah asked.

"Sorry." Shelley stepped aside and then closed the heavy wooden door behind them.

Cooler air welcomed them in out of the Texas heat. Above them, wide beams lined the cathedral ceiling of the entranceway, where a majestic staircase occupied one complete side. On the other side there was a large open-concept great room from where Hannah could glimpse a spacious kitchen and dining room.

The sound of a baby's whimpering led her to a small playpen that had been set up in the middle of the great room. Unable to help herself, Hannah picked up the child and held her close. Pushing damp curls from the baby's face, she was greeted with large brown eyes rimmed in red.

"It's okay, sweetheart," Hannah said as she instinctively began rocking the child in her arms as she checked her forehead for fever. "How long has she been crying like this?"

"She's teething. I've tried to give her that teething ring thing, but she just throws it down. I put some ointment on her gums about an hour ago," Shelley said.

"Poor baby." Hannah checked the baby's diaper.

"I know, it's so sad, isn't it?" Shelley said as she grabbed her book bag from the side of a chair.

"Sad?" Hannah asked as she lay Avery down on a nearby couch and peeled off her diaper. She took the clean one Lindsey handed her, along with wipes and a tube of diaper rash cream laid out on a side table. This really wasn't any of her business. Wasn't she involved enough, already?

"I mean, losing both her parents that way. My momma said it was a shock for Dr. Cooper, too. Losing his dad and stepmom like that and then finding out they'd named him as guardian of their baby if something happened to them. Major life change, right?"

"What?" Hannah paused for a moment. How had she not known that Dr. Cooper had recently lost his father and stepmother? Of course, the man had always been a bit quiet about his personal life. But still, he should have known that his coworkers would be there to support him.

And again, she reminded herself, this wasn't any of her business. If he didn't want anyone to know he had lost his father, she needed to respect his privacy.

She picked Avery up and hugged her close. This poor baby had lost her mother and father. The pain of her estrangement from her own parents still clung to Hannah after twelve years. Except, Avery's parents hadn't turned their backs on her like Hannah's had done the first time she'd gone against their wishes. They'd been taken away. Luckily for this child, she had a stepbrother who was there for her.

"Yeah, he went from Avery's half brother to pretty much her daddy in just a few days." Shelley glanced down at the phone in her hand then swore. "I've really got to go. I'm going to be so late." She started for the door then stopped and turned back. "I really appreciate this. I was feeling really bad because I knew Dr. Cooper didn't have anybody else to help with Avery."

"I'm sure there are a lot of people at work who would've been happy to help out if they'd known about Avery. The staff on my unit are always there to support each other. We just didn't know."

"That's good, because I was really dreading telling him that I couldn't help out anymore. He's a really nice guy and my mother loves working for him, but I have to put my classes first. I'm sure he'll understand. I feel so much better now that I know you'll be here," Shelley said.

Hannah watched as the girl hurried out, trying to understand what Shelley had meant. Surely she couldn't have thought that Hannah was going to...

"Shelley, wait!" Hannah called out as she heard the front door slam.

She set the baby inside the playpen and turned to Lindsey. "Stay here with Avery," she said as she ran from the room.

"Shelley," Hannah called again, rushing

out the door. Stopping in the driveway, she watched the bright red Mini Cooper drive away.

That girl was as fast as a Texas jackrabbit.

So many things had just happened that it took a few minutes for Hannah's brain to catch up. Dr. Cooper had recently lost his father and stepmother. Little Avery, who was Dr. Cooper's half sister, was now his responsibility. That had certainly been a surprise, though it helped to explain a lot of the man's behavior earlier that day. And then last, but in no way the least important, Dr. Cooper's babysitter, the only one he had been able to find, had somehow gotten it into her head that she wouldn't be needed any longer.

Walking back into the house, baby giggles and the laughter of her daughter echoed throughout the great room and soothed away the stress that had filled Hannah just moments earlier. It was going to be all right. In a city as big as Houston, there had to be someone Dr. Cooper could hire to take care of his little sister.

Looking around the rooms, she noticed the pile of dirty dishes in the kitchen sink and the trash can overflowing with diapers.

"Come on, you two, let's go explore this house and find this little one's room so we can get her cleaned up. We have a lot to do before Dr. Cooper gets home."

And she would have a lot of explaining to do if Shelley had really meant she wasn't coming back.

CHAPTER TWO

THE GARAGE DOOR slowly opened as William ran his hand through his hair. It had been a long day that had started with Avery waking him up before five in the morning, had continued through hospital rounds and office exams, ending with an emergent surgery that had proved he was clearly not prepared for all the changes Avery was bringing into his life.

He pulled the car into the garage, put it in Park and shut the engine off. Resting his head on the steering wheel, he took a minute to collect himself. Closing his eyes, he dragged in a deep breath and let it out slowly on a sigh derived from all the challenges of his day and the comfort he felt now that he was home.

A twinge of guilt worked its way into his subconscious as he tried to clear his mind. He'd been overwhelmed when Hannah had offered to rescue him. It was because of her that he had been able to save Mrs. Nabors from permanent neuro damage. He should get out of the car, go inside and thank her. Then she could get back to whatever she had planned for the night. But instead, he sat there, enjoying the first moment of peace he'd had all day. He needed this one moment before he could deal with whatever would be waiting for him in what had once been his quiet refuge.

It had only been a week since he'd received the call that both his father and his father's latest wife had been killed in a car accident. Three days since he'd learned that his father and stepmother had named him guardian of his half sister. Three days since his whole life had turned into a disorganized nightmare. What could his father have been thinking? Maybe, like him, he'd thought he would live forever?

William had no idea what it was he was supposed to do with the little girl. His only thought had been to call his housekeeper, who had six children and several grandchildren. Luckily, Angela's daughter had been happy to help him out for a few days while he looked for some permanent care. But Shelley was a busy premed student who was simply doing him a favor, not a professional nanny. Thank goodness, Angela would be here tomorrow to clean and do the laundry—and hopefully help him sort out the mess Avery's sudden arrival had brought into his life.

He glanced down at the crushed banana stain on his shirt. Avery had left it that morning when he'd tried to hand her over to Shelley. For some reason, the child had become attached to him the moment the former nanny had put her in his arms. It was like somehow, instinctively, she knew the two of them were in this together. Sink or swim, they were all each of them had now.

Of course, William had done more sinking than swimming in the last three days. And today, having Shelley say she couldn't stay while the OR was calling on the other line telling him his patient was ready for surgery, he'd almost gone under for the last time. He'd been afraid of just losing it in the middle of the lounge—something he had never done before—only to be saved when Hannah had offered a helping hand.

What would he have done if she hadn't

been there? He couldn't depend on others for last-minute help. He needed a better plan. He'd call all the agencies in the morning to at least assign him someone for emergency coverage until they found him some full-time help. It was impossible for him to believe that the top agencies in town couldn't recommend someone. Or maybe he should consider hiring a live-in caregiver. That would be the smart thing to do. That was what his own father had done when he'd found himself alone and responsible for a nine-year-old.

And look how well that turned out for you.

He pushed the gibe at his lonely childhood away.

This wasn't about him. It was about his half sister. He had to do the right thing for Avery. Only, he found himself floundering with every decision he needed to make. And the call he'd received from his lawyer today regarding Avery's great-aunt's inquiry wasn't making things any easier. What if, as the woman had claimed, the best place for Avery was with her mother's aunt? How was he supposed to know?

William had to come out from under the fog he'd been in since his father's funeral. It had been a week and it still didn't seem real to him. While he and his father had not been close, it was still hard to believe that the man he had grown up thinking was larger than life…was gone. Maybe it was the fact that his father's death had been just as sudden as William's mother's. It didn't seem fair, but he knew from experience that life never was.

What William really needed was to take some time off, but with one of the neurosurgeons out on maternity leave, that was not an option. Somehow, some way, he would make it through another night. Eventually he'd find the right person to care for Avery. He couldn't give up now. It had been what his father and stepmother had wanted. He had to make this work.

Hannah stood in the kitchen of her dreams as she browned the meat to add to the sauce she eyed as it bubbled on the chef-quality stove. She also kept trying to glance at the open pharmacy book she'd laid off to the side, trying to review classes of antibiotics. If she was lucky, she'd make it home in time to give the subject a good hour of study before she went to bed. Of course, given the day she'd put in, she'd probably fall asleep at her kitchen table again.

After taking care of Avery, she'd called everyone she could think of who might be able to help with Dr. Cooper's childcare issue. Not one person had been available for tomorrow. Stopping the search, she'd started dinner. Now, with Lindsey doing her homework at the marble-topped island that spanned almost the length of the large kitchen, she found herself worrying about what the doctor would do if Shelley didn't show up the next day.

Maybe if he called Shelley's mom, he could arrange things. That voice in her head had been right. She should have stayed out of Dr. Cooper's business. She had enough on her plate without worrying about other people's problems. But still, Hannah had been where he was and the only thing that had saved her from losing her job or missing a class was someone giving up their time to help her. She might even have missed being with her daughter for her transplant surgery if it hadn't been for Sarah, the nurse practitioner on the floor, coming to get her.

The sound of the garage door opening sent her thoughts back to the meal she was preparing. Somehow, she didn't think that her offering of pasta and sauce was going to help when he learned there wouldn't be anyone arriving to take care of Avery in the morning.

Hannah tried to make herself smile before the door that led to the garage opened, but it was impossible. There was no way this could go well. She'd be lucky if he ever talked to her again. And she'd miss that. He was one of the few doctors happy to let her pick his brain—pun intended—when something new came up at work.

He walked in and any bravado she had managed to collect disappeared. He stood a head taller than Hannah and what had earlier felt like a spacious room now seemed to shrink with his presence. She hadn't ever noticed how tall he was or the width of his shoulders. It was one thing to see him at work where he blended in with all the other staff members, it was another to be standing in his kitchen. *His* kitchen, which she had pretty much taken over.

"I'm sorry, Dr. Cooper. I hope you don't mind that I went ahead and started something for dinner. I wasn't sure how long you'd be in surgery," she said, busying herself stirring the sauce while fighting the awkward feeling of being somewhere she didn't belong.

"You're standing barefoot in my kitchen, cooking something that smells delicious, and you saved my life by coming here to take care of Avery. I think you can call me William," he said as he looked over her shoulder, his nearness setting off warning bells. Whether it was the heat from the stove or the heat of his body, she wasn't sure, but something had sent the temperature rising in the room.

"I wouldn't say I saved your life," Hannah said. The man saved lives daily with his surgery skills. All she had done was help out a coworker.

"You did me a big favor. Thank you," he said. "I owe you one."

"You don't owe me anything. I was glad to do it," Hannah said, though she did let the idea of the neurosurgeon owing her a favor roll around in her head. She really did need to find a good doctor to precept with. Maybe later, when he didn't have so much to deal with, she would ask him to be her teacher.

"Avery?" he asked as he bent over the pan of sauce.

"Fed, bathed, and down for the night. Her

bottom's a little red, but I covered it with some salve," she said. Standing close to him, she couldn't help but notice his body relax. It must be hard for him to go through all the changes in his life all alone. Now, she was going to make it harder when she reported that his babysitter likely wasn't coming back.

"You got her into bed?" he asked.

"Yes. She was worn out, poor thing. Shelley said she'd been fussy all day. I found some teething medication for her gums in her room and it seemed to help," Hannah told him.

"I owe you again, then. I haven't been able to get her to sleep unless I hold her. As soon as I put her down, her eyes pop open and I have to pick her up. I'd finally given up on putting her in her own bed. I just started sleeping in the recliner with her," William said.

"Hey, Dr. Cooper. So your real name is William?" Lindsey asked, looking up from her book.

"Good evening, Lindsey. And yes, my name is William. Why?" he said as he stepped away from Hannah.

"Does anyone ever call you Bill or Billy?" Though they had met at several of the department gatherings, Hannah had noticed that Lindsey had seemed very interested in the doctor today. She had been full of questions about him during Avery's bath time.

"No. Just William. Why?" He moved to the fridge and pulled out a bottle of water.

"I just think Billy the Brain Surgeon has a great sound to it. Don't you?" Lindsey quipped before returning her eyes to her book.

"How much to keep that moniker quiet around the hospital?" he asked Hannah, pinning her with a stare before a smile broke over his face.

He really was a handsome man with those startling pale blue eyes and thick brown hair curling at his neck. Put him in a pair of shorts and a T-shirt and he'd look like one of those California surfers.

"I think we can work something out," she said. "I do need to talk to you after I get supper finished."

"My momma was going to be a brain surgeon, too," Lindsey said, never looking up. "But then I was born with a bad heart and she had to quit college to take care of me. Now she has to be a nurse instead."

"Lindsey, why would you say that? I'm very proud to be a nurse." Hannah was shocked that her daughter would think such a thing.

Lindsay shrugged her shoulders as if it was no big deal, but they would definitely be having a conversation later.

No matter how the birth of her daughter had changed her life, Hannah would never let her child bear that burden. Interestingly enough, it sounded exactly like something her parents would tell their granddaughter. Perhaps it was also time for Hannah to have another talk with them.

Hannah had finally allowed her parents contact with Lindsey after years of their ignoring their daughter and granddaughter. At the time, their insistence that Hannah go to medical school had almost separated her from her daughter when Lindsey was born. She wouldn't allow them to put that type of pressure or guilt on Lindsey. She certainly wasn't about to let them start playing games with her daughter's mind. She would have no problem cutting them out of her life, just as they'd had no problem cutting a nineteen-year-old single mom and a newborn baby out of theirs.

"Well, I'm sure your mother would have

made a great brain surgeon, but being a nurse is just as important as being a doctor. Just this afternoon, she noted a change in one of our patients that was a sign something really bad was happening inside her head. If she hadn't observed the patient as well as she did, the woman might have had a very disastrous outcome," William said.

"That's awesome, Mom." Lindsey smiled at Hannah over her schoolbook.

"You are still young enough to go back to school, you know," William said, returning his attention to Hannah. "I had a professor who didn't finish college till he was in his late fifties. You're definitely smart enough and you have excellent instincts."

Hannah felt her face flush with his praise. She didn't know what to say. Being a nurse practitioner in a neurosurgeon's practice might not be the dream she'd had when she was younger, but it was close. And whether her parents agreed with her choices or not, she'd rather be a nurse and have her daughter than be the most sought-after neurosurgeon in the world.

"Maybe someday," Hannah said, not wanting to go into all the reasons why she couldn't make full-time schooling a reality right now. With a mountain of hospital bills from Lindsey's transplant operation and the student loans she had taken out for nursing school, it would be years before she could drag herself out of debt.

"But she's going to become a nurse practitioner instead," Lindsey said. "Grandmother doesn't think that's as good, but I do."

Hannah had known it was her mother who'd been filling her daughter's ears with rubbish. Definitely time for that talk.

"A nurse practitioner sounds like a great job for your mother," William said before turning back to Hannah. "Are you going to continue on the neuro unit at the hospital?"

Could she tell him that her biggest dream was to assist the best neurosurgeon in Houston? Him.

The *Star Wars* theme suddenly filled the kitchen and William reached into his pocket and pulled out his phone. "Excuse me," he said as he pushed the talk button and moved toward the stairs.

Finding a set of dishes in the cabinet, Hannah took a few minutes to fix Lindsey a plate of pasta and meat sauce. Setting it in front of her, she turned and was surprised to see William had returned. He'd changed into a pair of khaki pants and a clean button-up shirt of light blue that almost matched the soft blue of his eyes.

"That was my housekeeper, Angela, who wanted to make sure I knew her daughter wouldn't be here in the morning. She says Shelley told her that I'd found a friend to help out with Avery, so I wouldn't be needing her anymore."

"Yeah, about that Dr—I mean William..." Hannah set the dishrag down beside the sink. If there was a contest for someone screwing things up for themselves, she'd be a top contender. All hope of asking the man to help her get the clinical hours necessary for graduation disappeared. "Maybe we should step into another room," she suggested, looking over at Lindsey.

With a raised eyebrow, William motioned for her to follow him along the short hallway beside the front staircase. Opening a door, he stepped back so that Hannah could enter what appeared to be his home office. A large chair sat behind an even larger oak desk in the center of the room. In front of the desk sat two leather chairs, which looked very inviting after spending the last fifteen hours on her feet.

Hannah took a seat and waited. She knew that he couldn't really be angry with her. It had simply been a misunderstanding that had caused the girl to quit. That could be fixed. Right?

Shutting the door behind him, William leaned against it as he looked over at Hannah. From what Angela had said, he could tell something had happened to give Shelley the idea that she wouldn't be needed anymore. Thank goodness her mother had called to confirm the information. The last thing he needed was to get ready for work in the morning only to find he had no one to watch Avery. Now he just needed to find out what had really happened.

"Hannah, relax. I don't know what gave Shelley the idea that I didn't need her anymore, but I'm sure it was some misunderstanding," he said, trying to keep the stress out of his voice. He was exhausted. Between long hours at work and even longer hours at home with Avery, he was running on empty.

Three days and his whole life had been totally uprooted by one child who hadn't even had her first birthday. What would the next seventeen years be like? His heart rate shot up.

"Well…" Hannah said.

William watched as she rose and stepped closer to his desk, her back to him. His highest priority right now should be finding a live-in caregiver, but the thought of someone he didn't know being in his house didn't appeal to him. It wasn't that he didn't like people. He just liked his own space and privacy—something he would never have again.

No, that wasn't true or fair to Avery. He couldn't blame the child for interrupting his life after her own life had changed forever with the death of her parents. She was so young to have to go through this. Was she better off without the memories of what she had lost, though? He knew the pain of memories of someone close to him being taken away. He didn't want that for his half sister. Neither did he want her raised by nannies and stepmothers—people paid to care for her. But what was the alternative?

Not moving from the door, he returned

his attention to the woman in front of him. He'd always liked Hannah. She was known throughout the neuro unit as not only a talented nurse, but also a compassionate one. She was a pretty, bright, responsible woman and, from what he had seen of her spunky daughter, an excellent mother. But today Hannah had been more than that. She'd been a friend who'd stopped everything in her life to help him. After tonight, it would be hard to think of her as just a nurse he worked with. He found himself wanting to listen to her explanation of what had transpired with Shelley.

"Can I ask you a question?" Hannah said as she turned to face him.

"Of, course." He leaned further back against the door and crossed his ankles.

"When you hired Shelley, did you interview her?" Hannah asked. She'd apparently worked off whatever nerves that had been driving her and had come to lean comfortably against his desk.

"I'm afraid I wasn't given the type of warning that would allow me that luxury. I called the only person I thought might know someone who could help me," he said.

"But you didn't actually talk to her yourself

before you left her with Avery?" she asked in a voice that didn't hide her disapproval.

"Like I said, there wasn't time. Angela has been my housekeeper for over two years now. She has kids. She knows what kids need. I don't," he said. A bit of unease settled in his stomach. Had he left Avery with someone who had put her in danger? "Did something happen to Avery?"

"No, of course not. Shelley is a bright young girl who would be great as a fill-in babysitter for date night, but her life is too busy with her classes right now and that's her priority." Hannah added, "I'm pretty sure taking care of Avery was the last thing she was interested in."

"It's okay, Hannah. I know Shelley wouldn't work out in the long run. Her classes do have to come first. I understand that. I just don't understand why she thought I didn't need her anymore."

"Well, that's kind of my fault…" Hannah hedged. "When she told me about your parents passing—"

"My father and stepmother," he amended.

"Yes, and I am so sorry to hear that, William." Hannah's eyes shone with a genuine sympathy that he had seen in only a few of the people attending his father's funeral service.

"Thank you," he said, raw pain eating at him, though he couldn't understand where it came from. It had been years since he'd been close to his father. Why was he feeling so much now?

"So…" Hannah continued, "I told her that I wasn't aware of that or that you had a baby sister to take care of. I explained to her that if we, the staff at the hospital, had known, we would have offered to help. I think she took that to mean her help wasn't necessary any longer." She paused. "I really didn't mean to mess things up for you and Avery."

"I know you didn't. This is all just so new to me that I panic sometimes. I'm afraid I'll mess things up myself. I really don't know what I'm doing." Saying the words out loud, admitting to someone else his fear, seemed to quiet the angst that always seemed to lie right below the surface.

If he could just get one thing taken care of as far as Avery's childcare was concerned, he knew he'd feel better. Just having someone who knew what they were doing, someone with experience with a child Avery's age, would give him some small amount of comfort. At least then he would have someone to ask all the things he needed to know to be able to take care of the little girl. He didn't want to mess this up. He didn't want to mess Avery up the way his father had messed up with him. His father's answer had been to find a wife and a nanny and to leave William's care to them. That wasn't what William wanted for his sister. There had to be another way.

"Tell me something. Who takes care of Lindsey while you're at work? Or is she too old for a babysitter?" William asked.

"She thinks she is, but she's got another year before I'll be comfortable with her staying by herself," Hannah said. "She goes to after-school care provided at the school, and most of the time it works well with my schedule. I do have another mom who picks her up if I'm working late. Also, there's a group of mothers with children who have had heart transplants, or who are waiting for transplants, that's very supportive. We share childcare when needed."

"She's doing okay now?" William asked.

With the energy and spunk Lindsey had displayed earlier, it was hard to imagine her before the transplant. He felt a guilty punch to his stomach. Hannah had taken care of a child with a heart defect and had gone through the processes of transplant surgery, all, apparently, while studying and working. And here he was wallowing in feelings of incompetence? It was time for him to man up. He could do this.

"Oh, she's doing well now. It's a miracle the difference the surgery has made. I never would have dreamed that she could be as healthy as she is today," Hannah said, wiping at her cheek.

"I'm glad to hear that. It sounds like it's been hard on both of you," William said. He should say more, but what? He wasn't good at all this sharing of emotions. He cleared his throat. "So what is it you look for when you have to hire a babysitter?"

"Well, the first thing I look for is someone I can trust with Lindsey medically. She's old enough now that she understands how important it is to take her meds on time, and she's been taught the signs of early rejection, but I still want someone who knows what to do if there was an emergency.

"A lot of the teenage babysitting classes teach CPR now, which is wonderful and I know that there are day cares that require it." Hannah took a quick breath before continuing.

"Second, I check references. I need to know the person is responsible and has taken care of a child of Lindsey's age before. It's a lot different taking care of an infant versus an older child. Someone caring for a child Avery's age certainly needs to make sure that she's fed and clean, but Avery also needs playtime. It's very important for her development. And last, but still very important, I usually let Lindsey meet them before I hire them so I know it's a good fit."

"A good fit?" he asked. "Would that be a good fit with both you and Lindsey?"

"For a good working relationship, I think both the parent and the child should be comfortable with the caregiver. Of course, your needs are a bit different," she admitted. "What you really need is someone to help you become comfortable taking care of Avery. If you'd had other children, this wouldn't be a problem, but getting hit with all of this at once has to be challenging— N-not that you're doing anything wrong," she stammered. "I didn't mean that."

"It's okay. I'm the first person to admit that I'm struggling," he said.

He'd tried to explain to Avery's former nanny that he didn't know anything about babies, but the woman had refused to listen. It had only taken Mrs. Adams five minutes to inform him that his sister was his responsibility and that since he was a brain surgeon, he certainly should be able to figure it out. She'd then handed him Avery and stomped back to her car. How the woman had thought being a neurosurgeon was going to help him with caring for his sister, he didn't know. Was he supposed to suddenly understand childcare because he had a doctorate?

Hannah didn't seem to expect that from him. She understood. She'd said exactly what he'd been thinking all day.

He needed someone to walk him through this whole process of taking care of a child, and he now had a good idea who that person should be. He needed a teacher, and Hannah had all the qualifications. Not only did she understand how demanding work in healthcare could be, she also understood the inherent challenges. Plus, there was the added bonus that he was comfortable around Hannah. She didn't make him feel self-conscious. And if Maria, Avery's great-aunt decided to protest his custody, he needed to be able to show the courts and children's services that he knew what he was doing. Hannah could help him prepare for that. There couldn't be anyone better to help him with Avery than Hannah. But how could he ask her to help him when she already had more than anyone else could handle between her job and caring for Lindsey? Was there some way that he could help her?

"I know the perfect person for the job," he said as he pushed away from the door. He'd find some way to make things easier on her if she agreed to help him. "You do?" Hannah asked, relief in her voice.

This woman who had only spent a few hours with Avery really was worried about the child's care. More proof that he was making the right decision.

"I do. She meets all the qualifications," he said. "It's been proved that we work well together, and she would be a great help in teaching me all the things I need to know about taking care of Avery."

"That's wonderful. I'm so relieved. I've checked with all the moms I know and no one knew of anyone that was available," Hannah said. "Who is it? Do you think she could start tomorrow?"

"There's only one person I know who would be the perfect person," William said. "And that person, Hannah, is you."

CHAPTER THREE

"I CAN SEE the wheels turning in your head," he said then took a bite of pasta.

"And exactly what part of the brain would you call the wheels, Billy the Brain Surgeon?" Hannah asked. She watched him flinch as he washed the pasta down with some wine from the bottle he had insisted on opening. The man was apparently not used to being teased.

After William had shown Lindsey where she could watch her favorite sitcom and she'd assured herself that Avery was still sleeping, she'd listened to his sales pitch for fifteen minutes before she'd gotten tired of shaking her head and had decided that what they both needed was to eat. Thinking that, maybe with a break, she could get him to understand just how wrong she was for the job. Oh, she'd definitely been impressed by the figure he had quoted her. If she had known that taking care of rich people's kids paid so well, she could have done that instead of waiting tables before she became a nurse. She wondered about William's background that he could fling numbers like that out without wincing at least a bit.

But that wasn't what had her "wheels turning" right now. He wasn't the only one who could come up with a great plan. Her mind was quickly formulating one of her own. What was really giving her pause, though, was the fact that his suggestion could be a way for her to clock those necessary clinical hours. She was so close to finishing her college courses and she had always dreamed of working in the neurosurgical field. She just needed hands-on preceptor hours, and it would be a bonus for her to work with someone with his reputation.

"Let's say I do agree to this. What would be my hours?" she asked.

William picked up his napkin—one of the cloth ones he'd pulled from a drawer before opening the wine—and wiped at his mouth, bringing her attention to lips that were turning up in a slight smile.

She was amazed at the difference she could see in the man now. It was like he was a different person here in his home. In just the few moments they had talked alone in his office, something had changed between them. They'd had many discussions at work, and even on the occasional outings with their peers, but there had never been a personal connection. Hannah could easily see now that the two of them would work well together.

But still, she needed to consider every aspect of William's plan—a plan that depended on her. There was some pressure knowing that he and Avery truly did need some help, but she could only make the decision that was best for her and her daughter right now. Lindsey would always be her first priority.

"I need someone to take care of Avery while I'm at work, but I wouldn't expect you to do that. What I really need is someone who could live here and teach me what I need to know to take care of my sister. My stepmother's aunt, who raised her, is making noises about protesting my custody of Avery. My lawyer doesn't think it will ever make it into court, but I need to be prepared," William said as he pushed his plate away.

"Why would she do that? You're Avery's half brother. That makes you her next of kin," Hannah said. Anyone who had just been handed a child to care for would be in the same situation. He just needed some time, a little education, and hands-on experience.

"It's still a possibility," William said, "and if it comes to that, I want to be ready."

"But you want someone to live here? That would mean leaving my apartment and moving Lindsey in here with me," she said as she saw the hope for the plan circle the drain.

How was she supposed to ask Lindsey to move again? They'd moved four times since coming to Houston. Sometimes the moves had been a step up in living arrangements. Sometimes a step down. This would definitely be a step up, even though the apartment they lived in now was the best place they had ever lived. Besides, living off someone else was not the kind of thing Hannah wanted to teach her daughter. She'd fought hard for her independence and she wasn't about to give it up.

"Of course, I would cover the expense of the housing that you would still have to pay and, of course, as I told you earlier, I'd pay for your time." He rose from the table and took his plate to the dishwasher before returning for hers.

"I can't make a decision like this without talking to Lindsey, but I have a proposal of my own," she said, rising and moving to the cupboards to put things away as she went.

Was she crazy to even consider his offer? It would definitely make finishing school this semester easier. She might have to take an educational leave of absence from work, but she had enough saved to cover her expenses. It would be worth it to get to work with him. Being able to put that she trained under Dr. William Cooper would help her get into any neurology practice in the state.

"Whatever it is, I know we can make it work," he said as he wet a dish rag and began to wipe the counters. At least he didn't seem like one of those men that would expect her to wait on him. There was no way that would go over well.

"I'm about to finish up my nurse practitioner program at school, but I still need a lot of clinical hours before I can graduate. How would you feel about me working with you to get them? In exchange, I would be happy to help you become comfortable taking care of Avery on your own," she said, then held her breath.

If he agreed, her life would be so much easier. She could finish her semester strong and still be able to pay the bills and spend the time she needed with her daughter. "We could have an exchange of knowledge. How about for one month during the day you teach me everything I need to know to work in a neurosurgeon's practice and at night I'll teach you everything I know about raising a little girl?"

"That seems fair to me. Of course the first thing you'll need to teach me is how to choose a day care for my sister. I think I've already proved that I don't know what I'm doing as far as that is concerned," William noted.

"Then that's where we'll start. We'll go through a list of day cares together and pick the best one for Avery," Hannah said. Was she really going to do this? "You need to know that I haven't ever done anything like this. The only child I really have experience with is my own."

"You've done a great job with her and

you're a single parent. That's the kind of help I need. I need to learn how to do this all on my own." William leaned against the island, the stress he'd showed earlier gone.

"Just so you know, I'm definitely not Mary Poppins. Don't expect me to break out in song or to dance a jig." She demonstrated a two-step she'd learned as a child in tap dancing class.

William laughed and she was struck once more by the difference in him here in his home compared to how he was at the hospital. "I'm not sure about that. I think you've got a shot at it."

"That's because you haven't heard me sing," Hannah said. Thank goodness her parents hadn't seen the point of voice lessons.

"Want to shake on it?" he said, holding his hand out to her.

The voice of her mother telling her to slow down and to make sure someone wasn't taking advantage of her made Hannah hesitate a moment. He was certainly quick to agree. She couldn't help but feel that she was falling in with his wishes a little too easily. Memories of living with her parents and their constant manipulation had her holding back and second-guessing herself. Was there anything for William to gain besides the care of his sister?

If there was, Hannah couldn't see it. She'd made sure they had an agreement that benefitted both of them and she believed his intentions were pure. She had to quit being so suspicious of everyone. This was a deal that put the two of them on equal standing. And it was a good thing, too. It had only taken a moment for his little sister to wrap her fingers around Hannah's heart. She wouldn't have been able to walk away without making sure the child was cared for properly.

"Unless Lindsey has a problem with it, I think we can make it work." She stretched her hand out and felt the warmth of his fingers as they slid through hers then folded around her hand. Their palms sealed the agreement, but still her hand lingered inside his a moment longer than necessary. Pulling back, she slid her hand against her jeans-clad thigh to ease the disturbing tingle from William's touch. How had a simple sign of an agreement turned into such an intimate touch? This new William, the relaxed, more easy-going William, seemed dangerous. She started to tell him that she had changed her mind, that this might not be a good idea, but realized she couldn't do that without admitting how much his touch had affected her.

"The movie's over. Can we go home now?" Lindsey asked as she came into the kitchen.

"What?" Hannah queried, still rattled by her body's response to William's touch.

"Lindsey, we were just about to come get you. I thought you and your mom might like to see my video gaming room," William said.

Hannah watched as her daughter's eyes widened and knew that everything was already settled. There was no way her daughter would turn down staying at William's place now. It looked like the next month would be an adventure for them all.

By the time they walked into William's house, each carrying a box, Hannah was having serious second thoughts. It had been harder than she had anticipated to lock down her apartment for the next month. While it was in no way as grand as William's home, she had worked hard to reach a financial position that could afford them a nice place to live. For Hannah, it was a true testament that she could make anything she believed in happen. Even Lindsey had been a little down when they'd left their apartment, but by the time they'd arrived at William's home, her daughter's natural good mood had returned.

With Avery down for a nap and Lindsey off to unpack, Hannah went to put away her own things. Opening one of the double doors to the room where she would stay, she was taken aback by its size. She could fit half of her whole apartment into the one room. She walked to the wall of windows and opened the blinds to a view of the large lake for which the neighborhood had been named. It was a beautiful sight; the rolling, manicured lawn ending at a small pier that stretched across the shore. She could envision a picnic table spread with sandwiches and drinks. A yard set up for playing a game of croquet. And a family enjoying the nice spring day.

"Momma, come see what I've done to my room," Lindsey called from down the hall.

Turning, she found William leaning against the doorframe. "Will it do?" he asked.

"It's perfect, though maybe a touch too big. But I love the view," she said.

"I know. It was the lake that sold the house."

He moved across the room to join her at the window.

"But isn't the house a little big for just you?" Hannah asked. "Though it will be the perfect place to raise a family."

A shadow crossed his face as he looked away from her. She could almost feel the chill from the icy stare he shot through the window.

"Maybe it is a bit large, but I knew it was perfect when I bought it. It had everything I'd ever wanted, including this view. As far as the wife and two point five kids, that isn't in my future. A family is the last thing I planned for," he said before looking back at her.

"Why?" she asked. "Isn't that what everyone wants?"

"A wife and kids?" William scoffed. "It seems that what people want isn't always what they get. My father believed in that dream so much that he ended up having had four wives before he died. Maybe the fourth one was 'the one,' as they say. I hope so. But stepmom one and two were a nightmare that I would never want to repeat."

"I'm sorry to hear that. And I hope Avery's mom was the one, too." Hannah quickly turned her eyes toward the lake as a chill ran up her back. She'd been surprised at the bitterness in William's voice when he'd talked about his father and his father's wives, but she'd noticed that he hadn't mentioned his own mother. What part had she played in William's decision not to have a family?

But she had also detected sincerity in his tone and knew he believed what he'd said. The fact was he did have a family now, whether he accepted it or not. For all practical purposes, he was Avery's father as well as her brother. And Hannah had no doubt that someday he would add to that family. He just hadn't met the person he couldn't live without. It was the same for her, so she had no problem understanding where he was coming from.

As he turned and walked out of the room, she continued to stare at the lake. No matter what William might say, she was certain he had to feel a bit lonely when he walked around such a big house. The thought even made her a bit sad until she remembered that he wouldn't be alone any longer.

There was nothing like the laughter of a child to warm up a home, she thought, smiling to herself as she headed down the hall to Lindsey's room. William had said he wanted to learn everything he needed to know to take care of Avery. The first thing she would have to teach him was what it meant to be part of a family.

William took the steps down to the basement two at a time. The realization that he had said too much to Hannah had hit him the moment he'd seen the surprise in her eyes. If she only knew just how dysfunctional his family life had been while growing up, maybe she would understand that another family was the last thing he wanted. Yes, he had a sister now that he was responsible for, but that didn't mean he was going to fall for the whole happily-ever-after thing.

As always, dealing with other people's expectations for him to be the all-American family man stirred the demon inside him. Too often people assumed that because he was a single man he just hadn't met the right person yet. Women he barely knew tried to fix him up with their daughters or nieces. Coworkers hinted at other coworkers who would be happy to be involved with him. Even his patients seemed to find his single status anomalous, as if his marital state had anything to do with his talent in the operating room.

William had been given advice from more than one elderly man who had been married for decades. No one knew that he'd had all the family life he could handle with not one but three different stepmothers. He'd had enough family drama to last anyone a lifetime, and he had no intention of repeating his father's mistakes. For some reason, the man had never learned to live by himself. Well, he was not his father. William didn't need a woman in his life to make him happy. The whole reason for Hannah being there was so that he could learn to be an independent caregiver. His father could have saved himself a lot of heartache if he had only taken the time to learn that himself.

William walked into the bathroom where he kept a set of clothes for working out. In minutes, he was changed and in the workout room, pumping bars loaded with his maximum lift weight. He felt the irritation fade as he strained his body to its limit. He paced himself as he moved through the machines one at a time. His mind quieted with each repetition, and with the calm came the knowledge that he'd let old wounds push him into saying more than he should have to Hannah.

Why did everything feel so raw right now? The bandages he'd so carefully applied over the years were fraying, coming loose. With the death of his father, feelings and emotions he had held at bay for years were now surfacing. The arrival of Avery on his doorstep had not helped things, either, having disrupted the organized life on which he depended.

William had an orderly existence that he had been happy with for years. Now, things were changing, which was something he always had problems with. His life had transformed so much between one stepmother and the next that he cherished the comfort of the life he had made for himself. And now he was letting two more people into his life. Hannah and Lindsey. He knew Hannah was curious about him. He was curious about her, too. But expecting her to understand him was just too much to ask.

Excited to start her first day in William's office, Hannah was up early. After making sure that Lindsey was awake and getting ready for school, she'd helped William pack a bag for Avery, carefully going over every item that was needed. Though a little rusty at baby care, she'd quickly remembered the basics.

"Why do you count the diapers in the bag?" William asked as he scrambled an egg for Avery's breakfast.

True to his word, William had sat with her to go through the different day-care services with available openings in their infant/toddler rooms. She'd helped him weigh each of the day cares' pros and cons, and he'd picked a favorite that offered smaller rooms and a convenient location.

Of course, when she had explained that each child moved up to the next level of care according to their development, William had been certain that Avery would be advanced before any of the other children. That's when she'd noted the necessity of potty training. Pointing out that he had a little time until he would have to worry about it, he chose to put the lesson off. She didn't mention that by that time she wouldn't be around to help. There were just some things he would have to learn on his own.

"If you know how many you put into the

bag every day, you can tell how many times the day care is changing her," Hannah said as she settled Avery into the high chair.

"Shouldn't they do that without me checking on them?" William asked as he cooled the egg then cut it into smaller pieces that Avery could pick up with her fingers.

"I don't think there will be a problem, but it doesn't hurt to keep any eye on it yourself. Also, it's good to visit the day care at times when they aren't expecting you." Hannah tied a bib around Avery's neck, adding, "You've got this, so I'm going to check on Lindsey and finish getting ready."

After dropping Lindsey off at school, they'd arrived at the day care with a few minutes to spare and neither of them seemed to be in a hurry to go inside. Hannah couldn't help but worry about the little girl.

What if Avery thought they were leaving her just like her mother and father had the day they'd left her and never come back? Yes, children were very resilient, but the little girl had lost her mother and her father. Her world had been torn apart. She didn't have any way of knowing it wouldn't happen again. But then, did any of them?

Hannah's own daughter had lived one day at a time for years, and even now there was always the chance of her heart going into rejection. They both lived with that hanging over their heads, though they also chose not to let the fear ruin the life that they had now.

"You don't have to go in if you don't want to." William said as he opened his door.

"No, I want to go, too." Though she knew she should let him do it himself, she needed to see that Avery would be okay for herself.

Unable to wait any longer, she got out of the car and took Avery out of her car seat. Together, she and William walked into the daycare. You'd think the two of them were going to a firing squad by the way the two of them were acting.

She squeezed the wriggly little girl in a tight hug then handed her to William. "Avery, I have to go to work with William now, but we'll be back as soon as we can."

William took his sister and walked over to the teacher. After speaking a few minutes, he gave her a piece of paper and crossed the room to where the other children were playing.

With one more hug and a kiss on the Avery's soft, plump cheeks, he sat his sister on the rug with the other children. Rising, he stepped up to Hannah's side and they both watched as Avery immediately crawled to a toy train and began rolling it across the floor.

"It will get easier," Hannah said aloud, for both of them. She'd done this before with Lindsey, but she didn't remember it being so hard...though she was sure it must have been.

"She seems to be doing fine, though I don't really like the way that child—" William motioned to a curly headed little boy "—is eyeing her."

Hannah looked at the boy. He did seem to be sizing Avery up. "They'll be fine. It's her first day, so the other children aren't used to her. I bet by the time we get to the office she'll have made some new friends. Come on, big brother. We're going to be late for work."

William hesitated a moment before he followed her out of the day care. "It seems strange leaving her here by herself."

"I know, but it will be okay. What was on

the note you gave to the teacher?" Hannah asked.

"I gave her the number to the Operating Room and the Emergency Room in case they can't get me on my cell," William said as they got into the car.

"That was a good idea. I didn't think about you not being available. We did put down my number as a secondary number, but there might be someone else you'll want to change it to after I move back to my apartment," she said as he pulled out of the parking space and headed for the office.

"I'll need someone for emergencies for after-day care hours and, of course, I'll need someone for nights when I'm on call," William said. "Thanks for covering that while you're at the house."

"It's fine. And it will all work out. I've still got some contacts with people who helped with Lindsey. We'll find someone to help out on those nights."

"This single parent thing is a lot more complicated than I thought," he said as they turned into the office parking lot.

"It is, but if I could handle it, I know you can, too. Now, let's get inside, where you can start teaching me all the things I need to know to be the best nurse practitioner the neuro field has ever seen," Hannah said as she opened the door. Excitement began to race through her. This was one more step that would take her closer to her goal and she was ready to take it.

CHAPTER FOUR

HANNAH DECIDED THAT she would be glad when her orientation was over. She and William had agreed over dinner the night before that it would be a good idea for her to just orient herself to the running of his office before she started seeing patients with him.

Of course, he hadn't warned her about Nurse Marion. She had to hand it to the woman. She ran a tight ship. As soon as patients checked in at the front desk, they were taken for weight checks and vital signs measurements. Any changes since their last visit were recorded, as were medication updates. But that didn't mean Marion had to treat Hannah like she was a brand-new nurse on her first day of orientation.

Hannah knew how to interview a patient and she was more than competent at taking a patient's vitals. It didn't seem to matter that Hannah had been responsible for the care of some of the neuro patients in the hospital. Nurse Marion, as she liked to be called, was going to make sure Hannah's orientation was very thorough.

It was easy to see there was a bit of hero worship going on when it came to William and, if the woman were twenty years younger, Hannah suspected Marion would be crushing on her employer. Regardless, when William gave Marion an order, nothing could sway her from her duty.

Hannah thought she might pull her hair out before it was even lunch time.

"Marion, can I see Hannah for just a minute?" William asked, standing in the open doorway to his office.

"Certainly, Dr. Cooper," Marion said. "I'll go prep the next patient."

Hannah watched the woman head to the waiting room before saying, "Thanks for the rescue."

"You looked like you needed it. Marion can be a bit much, but she keeps this office running," William said before turning back to his office.

"She thinks a lot of you," Hannah replied as she followed him.

"She was the first employee I hired when I opened the practice. She's very dedicated." William took a seat behind his desk. "I checked on Avery and her teacher said she was doing fine."

"I told you she'd be okay. I'll call a little later to see how she's doing. That way it won't look like you don't trust them," Hannah told him as she looked at her watch. Though working with Marion had been trying, at least the time was passing quickly.

"Good, and thank you. I'll drop her off tomorrow by myself." William sighed. "None of this is going to be easy, is it?"

"Not really. It's always harder than you think it's going to be," Hannah said, "but you'll get the hang of it. What did I tell you was the first rule of parenting?"

"Don't let them see fear? I think it might be too late," William joked, smiling at her. "Knowing that you are looking out for Avery so I don't make any major mistakes means a lot, but I also know you have a child of your own and your courses. If it becomes too much, just let me know. Angela's at the house two days a week, so at least that's taken care of—"

The door to his office flew open. "I need you in the waiting room," Marion said before turning and running back to the front of the office.

Hannah and William rushed out behind her.

Hannah immediately recognized the young man on the floor. Zach had been in a car accident several months earlier and she had been his neuro nurse. Kneeling at his side, she noted that his eyes were open but not blinking, his muscles taut as violent spasms racked his body. Resting her hand on his chest as best she could, Hannah checked his breathing while William examined the bleeding cut on his head.

Remembering where she had seen the dressing tray, Hannah ran to the supply room and returned with some four-by-four gauze pads and wrap.

"Call 9-1-1 for an ambulance. Tell them he's having a grand mal seizure and I want him taken to the ER," William instructed

Marion in that calm voice that Hannah had always admired.

She felt Zach's body go limp beneath her hand and was relieved to see his chest rise with a deep breath.

"Will he be okay?" a voice asked.

Turning her head, Hannah saw Zach's wife, Sheri, standing behind her, eyes full of tears.

Hannah left the young man's side as Marion made the call and William rechecked his vitals. She knew how scary it was to watch a loved one suffer while their life was in danger. All you could do was stand on the sidelines and wait.

"Yes, he's going to be okay. He had a tonic-clonic seizure, what they call a grand mal. He could be out for a while now that it's over, but his breathing is good. See how his color is all pink? That's a good sign," Hannah reassured her as she took the woman's shaking hands. "Has he done this before?"

"No, nothing like this. He's had those small ones like he had in the hospital, but he's been taking his medication just like the doctor ordered," Sheri said, absently rubbing her small baby bump. She looked up at Hannah. "What if I had been at home alone? What would I have done?"

"You'd do just what we did—call 9-1-1," Hannah said, turning to look at William as he came up behind her.

The door opened to the waiting room and the few people in the waiting room stepped aside as two EMTs pushed a stretcher into the room.

"I've already called and talked to the doctor in the ER that will be taking care of Zach," he told Sheri. "They're going to take him to CT as soon as he gets there. I'll be in to see you and Zach as soon as the results are back." At her nod, William stepped away to talk to the EMTs.

For the next hour, Hannah and Marion worked hard to get the last of the patients seen before lunch so that William could leave to check on Zach. She couldn't hide her excitement when William invited her to accompany him. This was what she had looked forward to—being able to see the patient from the perspective of the doctor.

"Avery's teacher says she's doing great, by the way," Hannah said as she climbed into William's car. "There was apparently a tussle between her and a little boy when he tried to take a toy from her, but no blood was shed and Avery maintained her control of the fire truck. So, it's all good."

"Blood? Is she okay?" William asked with that deer-in-the-headlights look she had come to expect from him whenever they talked about his little sister. He was so scared he was going to do the wrong thing. He was like a new dad, only he'd missed the newborn stage that would've helped prepare him for what was ahead.

"I was joking. It was just two toddlers wanting the same toy," she said.

"Maybe I should go back to my original plan and call the agency to have someone come into the house." He maneuvered the car onto the road.

"Let's try this first. I really think it could be good for her to be around other kids her age. There were times when Lindsey had to have home care because of her medical condition. It was hard for her to watch all the kids out playing and not be able to join them. Which reminds me of something I wanted to ask you," she noted as they neared the hospital. "Does Avery have a pediatrician here in Houston?"

"Yes, I had Shelley take her to Dr. Anderson in the pediatric clinic. One of my father's lawyers had her pediatrician in Dallas email her records over. And yes, I know I should have been the one to take her," he said as he pulled into the staff parking lot at the hospital.

"We'll go together the first time. And it's fine if you need help sometimes. Just because you're going to be a single dad, doesn't mean you can't have some help from your friends." Hannah felt her heart squeeze. Hopefully, she would be one of those friends.

William was glad to see that Zach was awake when they walked into his room. The CT results had come back and, fortunately, there had been no damage as a result of him hitting his head on the office floor during the seizure.

"Hey, Doc," Zach said when he spotted them. "Hannah? It's nice to see you. Are you working in the ER today?"

"No, I've taken some time off so I can concentrate on school," Hannah said as they approached his bedside, "and Dr. Cooper is helping me get my clinical hours in neuro surgery. I was at the office today when you had your seizure."

"You're looking better than when we last saw you," William noted as he examined the sutures on the side of Zach's head. "How are you feeling?"

"I'm a little freaked out and very tired, to be honest," Zach admitted, reaching for Sheri's hand. "We both are."

"Did the CT show anything? He fell pretty hard. I tried to grab him," Sheri said, her voice breaking on a sob.

"It's not your fault, honey. There's no way you could have kept me from hitting the floor," Zach said then raised her hand to his lips for a kiss. "Besides, you have more than just me to worry about right now."

William looked away from the young couple. He'd never been one for public displays of affection. He heard someone sigh and looked over at Hannah, whose eyes were brimming with tears.

He leaned closer to her. "Do I need to get you a hankie?" he whispered, surprised to hear the tease come out of his own mouth.

"Even you have to admit that they're a sweet couple. They're going to make great parents," she said softly before sighing again.

William straightened and cleared his throat. "There's no change on the CT from the last one you had, but I want to admit you at least for one night. I'm going to adjust your dose of anti-seizure meds and hopefully that will take care of the problem. If not, we'll look at changing the medication to see if that helps. Right now, I want you to take it easy for the day and I'll—" he looked over at Hannah "—*we'll* be in to see you later."

They left the couple arguing about whether Sheri would spend the night at the hospital. William helped Hannah transcribed a note for Zach's chart and explained the admissions orders.

He wasn't surprised at how quickly Hannah caught on. She was smart and already familiar with the hospital's computer system. What did surprise him was how many of the ER nurses stopped to talk to her.

"Did you ever work in this ER?" he asked after another nurse stopped by.

"Worked here? No. Spent a lot of time here? Oh, yes. Before Lindsey received her new heart, she was in and out of the hospital so much that we both knew all the nurses."

"It must have been hard being a single parent of a child as sick as Lindsey," he said. He hadn't lasted three days with a soon-to-be toddler and that was with Shelley's help. He couldn't imagine what it had been like for Hannah all on her own.

He'd wanted to ask her several times about Lindsey's father, but as someone who wasn't comfortable with people querying his own private life, he didn't think it fair to ask questions about hers. Still, from what he had seen, Hannah had handled everything life had thrown at her and her daughter by herself. He just hoped he could do half as well with Avery.

CHAPTER FIVE

HANNAH FROZE, STUNNED by the sight in front of her. She needed a fan, a glass of water—anything that would cool her heated body and quickly.

Standing in the middle of the staircase that led into the basement, she had the perfect view of flexing muscles and a hard, bare chest that any man would be proud of. How had she not known what this man had been hiding under his lab coat?

Her breath caught as she watched William lift the heavy weighted bar over his head, giving her a view of sweat-drenched abs and a small line of hair that led to a pair of low-waisted gym shorts. She knew she couldn't just stand there and ogle the man, but her legs refused to continue down the stairs. And she certainly wasn't going to leave now. Her poor neglected body wouldn't have let her anyhow. It hadn't been this close to an undressed man, not intimately at least, in more than…was it four or was it five years? And she had never seen one like this.

A shudder ran through her as hot need settled in her lower abdomen and the parts of her body that she'd ignored for too long protested. Could a woman orgasm just by looking at a man? If it was possible, this would be the man that could make it happen.

The loud clang of metal brought her back to her senses just in time to see the man she was openly lusting after run a towel over tight, damp abs before moving to some type of leg machine that had him on his back. He started pumping strong thighs up then down.

Hannah realized she couldn't just stand there. At some point he would look over and see her, and there was no way she'd be able to hide the reaction that had taken control of her. She had two choices: sneak back up the stairs or walk down and face the temptation.

Who was she kidding? There was no way she was strong enough to leave now. She just had to make sure William didn't notice how the sight of all him hot and sweaty affected her.

She pushed back against all those long-ignored hormones fighting to free themselves. She could do this. She'd been without a man for a long time and survived. She'd just ignore him. It would be easy. All she had to do was to pretend he was naked...wait, what? No. God no, that was what you did if you were nervous giving a speech, not lusting after a man. It was hopeless. She needed to leave.

"Are you coming down or are you going to run away?" William quipped as he walked toward her.

She would have probably run if it hadn't been for the taunt in his voice. And was that a smile on his lips? In all the years she'd worked with him, she couldn't remember seeing Dr. Cooper smile like that. But this wasn't Dr. Cooper. This was William, and she had an uneasy feeling that this man was a lot more dangerous than the Ice Prince of the OR.

"I didn't want to disturb you." She forced the words out over parched lips. She really did need that glass of cold water. She remembered the monitor in her hand. "And you forgot this."

"Sorry. I haven't gotten used to needing a monitor yet. And you're not disturbing me. There's enough equipment here for two," he said before running the towel down the length of his body.

Hannah closed her eyes and bit down on her poor lip to keep a moan from escaping. Surely he didn't mean that the way it had come out. It had to be her sex-fogged mind that had turned his words into innuendo. She had to leave before she did something that would embarrass both of them. Hannah looked down at the baby monitor clenched between her hands. Water, she needed water.

She cleared her throat. "I'm going to run back up to the kitchen and get a bottle of water," she said and turned, fighting the urge to run.

"There's plenty in the fridge over in the corner. Hold on, I'll get you one," he said.

It was no use. The man was determined to torment her. It was okay. She deserved it. She should have run the moment she'd seen him. Instead, she'd stood there like a hormonal teenager.

Hannah walked down the stairs, reaching for the bottle of water he held out to her as she passed him. Twisting off the cap, she up-ended the bottle and drained half of it before pausing. She put the lid back on and then, straightening her back and holding her head high, walked to a stationary bike and sat the baby monitor and bottle of water down beside it. A few miles on the bike should be enough to cool her traitorous body down.

Four miles later, she was feeling much better. The bicycle faced a glass door that lead to the backyard and she'd forced herself to keep her eyes trained there. Behind her, bars and weights rattled and clinked together, but she refused to look over at the man who used them. By the fifth mile, the embarrass-ment was gone. Why was she feeling guilty of something? Okay, maybe she was guilty of a little innocent gawking. But if the tables had been turned, she was certain he would have done the same thing. Right?

And wouldn't it be fun to turn those tables on him? She waited for the voice inside her head to tell her not to do it. Apparently, her mother had been shocked speechless. It was a good thing, too, because Hannah had no intention of listening to her voice of reason.

William couldn't keep his eyes off the woman that had showed up in his home gym. Dressed in a tight exercise tee and shorts and sitting on the bike in front of him, he was tortured by every twist of her hips as she pedaled her way into dreams he had no business dreaming.

He'd taken her into his home and office, but he could not let her any closer. He had very precise conditions for the women he spent time with, and the first one they clearly understood was that there would be no happily-ever-after with him. He'd always been up front about that, and had otherwise provided them with all the things that he could give them. Yet Hannah was not the type of woman who would accept expensive jewelry or exotic trips instead of love and a future. He had neither of those things to give.

Dropping the weight in his hand, he reached for a towel at the same time Hannah stopped pedaling.

Good. Maybe now she'll leave.

He shouldn't have teased her, but when

he'd turned to see her standing there, a look in her eyes that invited him to take everything he wanted from her, he'd had to change the mood. He knew he'd embarrassed her, and had assumed she'd run. It wasn't until she'd marched down the stairs and mounted the bike that he'd realized his mistake.

A deep moan echoed across the room and he felt his groin tighten with the sound. Oh, he'd definitely made a mistake in teasing her. She stretched her arms up and arched her back, shaking out golden hair that hung down her back in thick waves. Thoughts of knotting his hand through those waves and baring her neck for his lips were enough to have him turning away from her and looking for his bottle of water.

He let the cold fluid run down his throat and then splashed some across his face. When he opened his eyes, he saw that Hannah had moved to the chest press. He watched as she propped one long leg on the seat and ran the towel up and down from ankle to thigh. She then repeated the process on the other leg before looking over at him.

"I'm sorry, did you want to use this?" she asked.

She wasn't playing fair and she knew it. He waited until she sat back on the bench and raised her arms to grab the handles before he pounced.

Hannah let go of the grin she had been hiding. She would have to be blind not to see that William had been just as affected by her as she had been by him.

Yeah, stud, let's see how you like it.

She felt the heat of his breath on her neck before she heard him.

"You're playing a very dangerous game, Hannah. You might want to make sure you understand the rules before you go any further."

She closed her eyes as his whispered words shivered down her spine. Her breath caught when she opened them. He was gone.

She waited until she heard his footsteps on the stairs before turning around. Her body trembled with a need she had never felt before her breathing was ragged and irregular. What had he meant? Games? Rules? The only thing that was clear was that he didn't play fair. She had only thought to get some of her pride back after being caught staring at him.

No, that wasn't true. She had wanted to see how he would respond to her. And he was right. She had no idea what the rules were for playing *games* with a man like William. But she was a quick learner when it came to something she was interested in. And she was finding herself more and more interested in this new Dr. Cooper. Besides, right now, they were just doing some innocent flirting. Lots of people flirted without things going any further. And if things did go further? Well, she'd worry about that later. What she needed was a cold shower, which had nothing to do with her workout.

William plowed through the long line of patients scheduled for the day. Unable to sleep the night before, he'd prowled the banks of the lake until early morning. He'd thought to scare Hannah off when he'd approached her with his words of warning in the gym. He'd wanted her to understand that she was playing way out of her league. Only, that wasn't what had happened. From the moment he'd caught her standing on those stairs with those deep blue eyes trained on him, he'd known that he was the one in trouble.

"Room three is ready," Hannah said from the open doorway to his office. "It's Mr. Mc-Grew. He's here for his post-op visit after his lumbar fusion. I went ahead and reviewed his range of motion. His pain scale is down and he's very happy with the results."

It was the most she had said to him since the night before. Even so, she still wouldn't look him in the eye. Was she embarrassed? Did he owe her an apology? They should probably talk about it. Women liked to talk about things. But how could they talk about it when he wasn't even sure what "it" was? All he knew was that he couldn't forget how Hannah had looked when she'd turned the tables on him. He'd taken two cold showers and still been up most of the night.

"Hannah, we need to talk." His phone dinged with the ringtone that notified him of a trauma in the ER. Reading the text message, he pushed back from his desk.

"Tell Marion to take care of the office. There's a trauma in the ER we need to go see," he said as he reached for his hospital lab jacket, already feeling his blood boil at the description of the patient's injuries and the ER doc's message that he was suspicious of the husband having caused them.

Domestic abuse. It never made sense. Why did men feel the need to mistreat the very women they'd promised to take care of? To love and to cherish? You didn't abuse someone you cherished. 'Til death do us part? In sickness and health? He'd learned from his father that those vows were just pretty words for a crowd of guests. By the time his father had wed his fourth wife, he'd proved that his vows meant nothing.

He had only been nine when his mother had fallen down the stairs and received a traumatic brain injury which had resulted in her spending the rest of her life in a nursing home. By the time he was ten, his father had divorced William's mother or wife number two and he was only a teen by the time wife number three had come into the picture. He couldn't help but presume that it had only been death that had stopped his father at wife number four.

A pang of sympathy slipped through the thick armor he had in place at the thought of the little girl he had been entrusted with.

His half sister would never know either of her parents. He knew Avery would miss her mother just as he had missed his when his mother was taken away from him.

The ride to the hospital was quiet. He'd given Hannah his phone to access the portal that contained the hospital's patient records as much to get her up to date on the patient as to keep her occupied while he dealt with his own demons. These types of injuries always brought out the worst in him.

They stopped at the ER desk to review the CT of the patient's head. From the ER doctor's description and the test results, it was easy to see the woman had a hairline skull fracture and possible concussion. She'd recover this time. It was the circumstances of the injury, however, that most concerned them. Next time she might not be so lucky.

"Let me go in first," Hannah said. "It might be easier for her to talk to another woman."

"Okay, see what you can get her to admit to. So far, she's claiming she tripped and fell. Maybe she'll relax around you," William said.

"It's worth a try. Good luck," the ER doc

said before he picked up a chart and headed off to see another patient.

While Hannah went to see the patient, William took a seat at the desk and searched the patient's records. He wasn't surprised to read that there had been more than one visit to the ER in the last six months with an injury that was always put down to some type of accident. On one visit, she'd claimed to have tripped over a basket of laundry. On another, a rug had caused the fall that had led to a sprained wrist and busted chin. Each time the staff at the hospital had tried to get her to admit that she had been abused, but the woman had always denied it, leaving their hands tied. She was just another example of misplaced love.

William heard the shouting and shot to his feet. He could hear Hannah's voice and that of an unknown male.

He found her standing outside a trauma room doorway, her body ridged and her head thrown back as she looked up at a large man who was over six feet tall. Was this the abusive husband? The guy raised his voice at Hannah. "That's my wife in there. You have no right to keep me away from her," he snarled, giving Hannah a nasty stare.

William stepped between the two of them as the man attempted to push past her.

"Hannah, go into the room. I'm sure this man understands that our patient needs some privacy while we examine her," William said, his tone cold yet calm even though he wanted to punch the man in the face.

Hannah's hand slid out to the man's arm and she pulled him aside as two hospital security officers approached.

Stepping in front of him, she lowered her voice. "I understand that you are upset, Mr. Jones, but we are just trying to do our job. Now, these two officers are going to find you a nice seat in the waiting room where you can wait till someone tells you that you can come back. If you choose to continue arguing with us, these officers will call the police and have you removed from the hospital. It's your choice," Hannah said.

The man settled down and the two officers escorted him from the ER with warnings of calling the police if he caused any more trouble.

"Now, if you'll let me do my job, I'll introduce you to Jeannine Jones," she said to William as she turned toward the trauma room. He followed her inside without saying a word.

What had he done? He'd only wanted to protect Hannah. To keep the man who he believed had beat his wife away from her.

A small woman was perched on the side of a stretcher. Dressed in a silk blouse and dress pants, she ran trembling fingers along the string of pearls at her neck. Her arm had been splinted, Velcro strips holding it in place. Her pale skin highlighted the long row of black stitches above her eye. Purpling bruises marred her forehead, contrasting with dullness of the blue eyes that stared up at him. All medical evidence suggested Jeannine Jones had been physically battered. In his mind, whoever had abused her deserved to be locked up.

"It's nice to meet you," William said, dragging his thoughts away from things he could not change. "I'm Dr. Cooper. I'm the neurosurgeon on duty today. Can you tell me what happened?"

"I've told everyone that it was an accident. I just tripped. I'm clumsy, that's all." The woman's eyes begged him to believe her.

What must her home life be like? he wondered, unable to even imagine the fear she might be living with day by day.

"I know it's frustrating, but it helps us in our neuro assessment," Hannah said, stepping closer to the stretcher. "Just like how we keep asking if you know your name and date of birth. With the injury to your head, we need to make sure your mental status doesn't become altered as that could be a sign of a much bigger problem." She took the woman's hand and held it comfortingly in her own.

"But I feel fine," Jeannine insisted, pulling her hand back. "I don't know why Tabitha called that ambulance. It was such a small cut."

"Is Tabitha a friend?" William asked. If anyone needed a friend, it was this woman.

"She lives next door. She comes over for tea sometimes when Calvin is at work. Calvin thinks she's a busybody, but she's really a very nice girl."

A nice girl who had taken on the duty of guardian angel to a woman who'd apparently been abused for too long, it seemed.

"Head wounds bleed a lot. It probably scared her to see the blood, and she did the right thing. You needed the stitches to close the gash above your eye," Hannah said. "Maybe we could call Tabitha and you could stay with her until you feel better?"

"No, I need to go home. My husband needs me there," Jeannine said, panic coming back into her voice. Panic and fear.

There was no way William was letting this woman go home today.

"Actually, I've reviewed the CT and there's a good probability that you have a concussion. I need you to stay overnight so we can make sure that you're okay. I know Tabitha would want you to stay," William said as he looked to Hannah.

"Wouldn't she feel better knowing you were doing what the doctor asked?" Hannah picked up his cue. "How about I call her so I can let her know you're doing okay? She's probably worried about you. If you give me the number, I can call her for you," Hannah said as she pulled her phone from her pocket.

William stepped out of the room to let Hannah work her magic as he knew she could. Jeannine wasn't ready to admit that she was being abused. Hopefully, her friend Tabitha would find a way to help the woman.

Within a few minutes, Hannah stepped out of the room.

"Did she agree to stay?" he asked as they made their way through the emergency department. "Was her friend helpful?"

"Jeannine has agreed to spend the night. Her nurse is going to take a guard with her when she goes to tell her husband in case he tries to cause trouble." Hannah added, "Her friend was out, so I gave Jeannine my cell number in case she needs anything."

"I don't understand how people let themselves get into this type of situation. It doesn't make sense. How can someone who says they love you hurt you like that? And how can you love someone who would do something like that to you?" William said. "Don't they see that that person is just using their love against them?"

"I wish I had the answer," Hannah admitted. "I'm sure love means different things to different people, but I know that what Calvin Jones feels for his wife can't be real love. Jeannine knows it, too. She kept saying how embarrassed she was, and I don't think she meant the injuries. I think she sees herself as weak and that's what she's embarrassed about."

"Then why doesn't she leave?" William asked as he opened the door that would lead them back to the parking lot.

"She probably doesn't feel like she can leave. It's scary being out on your own, William. They have no children and, if her husband is like most abusers, he's cut her off from her friends and family. I'm going to call the social worker on the neuro floor when we get back to the office to see if she can help."

Hannah opened the door to the car. "Maybe this time Jeannine'll reach out for help."

"I hope you're right," William said as he settled in behind the wheel and started the engine. "Because I have a feeling that the next time her husband decides to beat on her it might be too late."

CHAPTER SIX

STANDING AT THE kitchen window, Hannah watched William as he snapped his fishing line in the air above him before laying it precisely in the same spot over and over. He'd been out there for more than half an hour and she hadn't seen him pull in a single fish.

She was supposed to be studying while William and the kids played outside, but she had stopped for a moment to check on them and now she was unable to step away. The repetition of the movement was mesmerizing as he brought the line out of the water again and again, making it dance in the air above him before casting out once more. It was a beautiful sight and she was only watching for the elegance of the movements. It had absolutely nothing to do with the way William's body swayed with each cast, his muscles tensing as he whipped the line back then relaxing as he let it sink into the water. Nope, it had nothing at all to do with William.

Refusing to waste the precious time she had to herself, Hannah moved back to the table and settled down to study. She had no time to be gazing out the window. She had an assignment due before the weekend.

Only, being out of sight did not take the vision of William from her mind. Both the cool, calm and collected man who ruled the operating room and the man standing alone on the bank of the lake were fascinating. The more Hannah saw of him, the more questions she had. And it wasn't just the physical attraction she felt for William that had him constantly in her thoughts. The man was such a mystery that she felt the need to find out what had made him that way. How could he go from cold to hot so fast?

The sexual awareness between the two of them seemed to be increasing every day. At some point, one of them would make a move. When it happened, would they be risking their new friendship for something that could easily burn itself out? Would it be worth it? She remembered how William had looked just moments earlier. How his smile made the muscles in her stomach clinch and her breath catch. How the boyish grin he'd given her the night before while they'd bathed Avery had set her heart to racing. Would she have the strength to walk away from that man? No, she definitely would not.

"Mom, have you seen my video headset?" Lindsey asked as she rushed through the back door. "William says he'll play with me after he gets Avery to sleep since I've already gotten my homework done."

"I don't think I've seen it. Are you sure you brought it?" Hannah asked as she shut the textbook. She'd been reading the same paragraph over and over and still couldn't remember the information.

"Maybe it's in the stuff that I left in that black box by my desk," Lindsey said. "I get to choose the game so I have the advantage."

Hannah shook her head as Lindsey ran down the hall to their rooms. It seemed that every couple of days Hannah had to make a trip to their apartment to retrieve something one of them had forgotten.

Deciding she might as well take a break, Hannah put together some drinks and took them out to the backyard. Setting the tray on the picnic table, she reached into the playpen where Avery was playing. The wiggly girl clapped her hands then wrapped them around Hannah's neck.

Hannah's heart squeezed. The child was quickly working her way into Hannah's heart, right along with her brother. If she wasn't careful, Hannah would have her heart broken by both of them when she had to leave. Something she wasn't sure she could survive. Unfortunately, her heart didn't seem to understand the danger.

The lake was calm, the water lapping against the bank in a slow, steady rhythm that had always soothed him. Only, today, it did nothing to calm the anger he felt toward a man he didn't even know. Inside, he knew there was nothing more at the moment he could do in a case like Jeannine's, but that didn't make him feel any better.

William couldn't shake the picture of Jeannine Jones sitting in the emergency trauma room all battered and broken. How many times had she awoken from a beating and wondered where her life had gone wrong?

How many times had she regretted that she'd ever met her husband?

He looked back toward the house, relieved to see that Hannah had moved away from the window. He'd known she'd been watching him. He'd seen that window a hundred times from the banks of the lake, had looked out of it himself hundreds more, but never had it looked so right to see Hannah standing there. It made him think of things that could not be. Not for a man with his family's history of mistakes. William had sworn to his own father that he would never make the same mistakes his father had repeated over and over.

Still, the sight of Hannah in his kitchen window had seemed so right at that moment. She wasn't just the nurse or the student or the friend who was there to help him, though she was all of those things. She was the woman he had discovered that night in the gym, the one still giving him restless nights.

But what did she see when she looked at him? Was it the renowned surgeon or the wealthy bachelor? Avery's half brother? The doctor she worked with? Or did she see the man who had almost lost himself to the need she'd made him feel that night in the gym?

A need that tugged at him as she crossed the yard to him now.

"I thought you might need something to drink," she said, holding out a glass of what looked like lemonade. Taking the glass, he slowly sipped the tart yet sweet juice and then smiled at Avery as Hannah transferred her from one arm to the other. He was using the time to collect his thoughts from the dangerous ground where they had wandered.

"Thanks. I wanted to apologize for the way I acted today. I should have known that you could take care of yourself," he said, knowing he couldn't promise he wouldn't do the same thing again.

"I can take care of myself, William. I've been doing it for years. Calvin Jones isn't the first irate family member I've had to handle and he won't be the last. I'd already sent one of the techs to get the officers."

"I know you can handle it. I just lost it for a few minutes. All I could think about was how he had hurt his wife, someone he was supposed to care about. I figured he'd have no problem hurting you. But I should have known you were prepared," he conceded. "And you did a great job with Jeannine, too.

I checked on her before I came outside and the nurse said she was resting well."

"Thank you, William," Hannah said, looking out over the lake. "I'm glad she's doing well."

"There's something else I want to talk to you about…" William he rested his glass on the grass. "I got a call from one of my father's lawyers and it seems there are a lot of papers in my father's office I need to personally go through and decide what to do with. So I'm going to have to make a visit to my father's house this weekend." He began taking his casting rod apart. "I don't expect you to come with me. I know you have a lot of studying to do right now."

"And miss you experiencing a road trip with Avery? Never. Besides, I think it's a good idea to take her back to her home."

Her words startled him. "What?" he asked, his hand stilling above his tackle box.

"I realized, talking to Lindsey just now, how much stuff we left behind that we probably should have brought with us," Hannah said. "There are probably things at your father's place that Avery is attached to. It's kind of like me moving Lindsey in here. I let her make the decision about the most important items to her—what she couldn't live without, sentimental items—and those are the things she packed to bring here."

"Avery's not even one year old. There can't be much that she's attached to at her age," he quipped softly. Sentimental? A pre-toddler?

"And what about photos? Someday she'll want to see pictures of herself as a baby. She also needs pictures of her parents. Those are things she'll cherish when she gets older. Things that can't be replaced. Things she'll guard for the rest of her life."

He thought of the small box he'd hidden in the attic all those years ago. Was it still there? It had held nothing of any real value, only memories of the childhood he had lost. Memories of a mother who had been taken away from him. Like Avery's mother had been taken away from her. He and his baby sister had too much in common.

"I don't know what the plans are for your father's house, but this is too important to leave up to the staff that might not know what to keep for Avery," Hannah said, her chin rising as if readying for a fight. Did she think he wouldn't take her concerns serious?

William trusted that Hannah knew more about what his sister needed than he did. "Okay, I'll make arrangements and see if Avery's nanny can meet us there this weekend. I don't know if she's taken another job, but I'm sure she'll want to help if she's able to. Will that work for you?" he asked, glancing once more at the lake whose calm waves had always given him the peace he needed in his life.

Just the thought of returning to his childhood home caused his stomach to churn. With the way his life was changing, he had a feeling it would be many years until his life was peaceful again.

The fact that that thought didn't bother him as much as it had before Avery, Hannah and Lindsey had moved in with him scared him most of all.

Accompanying William on his rounds through the neurosurgery intensive care unit was one of Hannah's favorite things to do. Not only did she get to see all her friends and coworkers, she got to see the patients from a different perspective.

"Can you dictate the consult note?" William asked as they exited an elderly patient's room. The man had suffered a subdural hematoma after a fall and was being closely observed because of the anticoagulants he had been taking.

"Sure," she said as William approached the ICU doctor on staff for the day. The fact that he trusted her skills enough to take on the task made her smile as she took a seat at the nurses' station to type up her notes.

"So, what's it like to work with Dr. Frosty?" one of her coworkers said as she slid her chair over till it bumped Hannah's.

Kitty had a bit of a mouth on her, but Hannah knew she was meticulous in the care of her patients. She was also a friend who could always be counted on in a pinch. Should Hannah mention her current arrangement with William? It wasn't like they were keeping it a secret.

"Hush. He'll hear you," Hannah said, looking over to where William stood with the other doctor. "And it's great."

"You two certainly looked close," one of the respiratory techs said as she joined them.

"He's as great at teaching as he is at surgery. I couldn't have asked for a better preceptor." Hannah really wasn't sure what to tell them about William. He was a man who valued his privacy and she respected that.

Making a point to appear caught up in studying the patient's chart, she was glad when there were no more awkward questions. Eventually someone would see them together outside of work and the rumors would start. When that happened, she'd deal with it, but talking about William behind his back was not something she was going to do.

After completing their morning rounds, Hannah and William took the elevator to the parking garage. As the doors shut, she relaxed for a second. From patient rounds to surgery and then follow-up appointments, there just didn't seem enough hours in the day.

"Dr. Frosty, huh?" he asked as he leaned against the side of the elevator.

Hannah wished she could go through the elevator floor. Her face burned with embarrassment. Had Kitty's words hurt him?

"She didn't mean anything by it," Hannah said. What would he say if she told him she thought of him more as Dr. Hottie than Dr. Frosty after that night in the gym? They'd both chosen to pretend that nothing had happened that night, but she knew neither of them had forgotten it.

His lips quirked into a half smile. "I guess it's better than Bill."

"Or Billy? I just can't see you as a Billy. Though, like Lindsey says, Billy the Brain Surgeon has a good ring to it." Hannah laughed at his look of horror. She was finding out that teasing the always-so-serious doctor was a lot of fun. He was always so good-natured when Lindsey gibed him. It made him seem so much more human.

Her thoughts suddenly took an unprofessional turn as she took in the way he looked right then, his body relaxed, his whole attention on her, which always sent shivers running along her spine. But he had no way of knowing that.

"Did you manage to get in touch with Jeannine?" he asked as he looked away. She'd caught that look of frustration before he'd turned his head and had no problem understanding it. Finding out the abused woman had left with her husband before they'd made rounds, her self-discharged had been upsetting for both of them.

"I've tried to call, but I just keep getting sent to her voice mail," Hannah said, taking out her phone and checking once again.

William's phone dinged. The ringtone was one she had come to know meant an emergency. He checked it before moving to the elevator buttons and punching in the ground floor.

"'Motor vehicle accident victim with head injury,'" he read aloud. "'Positive for loss of consciousness. Twenty-nine-year-old male. No seat belt. In CT now.'"

The doors opened and they both headed for Radiology, only to learn the patient had been sent back to the emergency ward.

"I want to go talk to the radiologist. I'll meet you in the trauma room," William said to Hannah.

"Okay." Hannah reversed her course. She'd never worked in the ER, but she'd made many trips to the pediatric side of the unit in the past. She had a lot of respect for the staff who worked there. It took a special person to deal with everything that walked through the doors.

The trauma room was crowded with medical staffers. The first thing she noticed was a nurse starting the rapid transfusion pump. That was a bad sign. The young man was bleeding from somewhere, which would make an emergent surgery even more complicated if he also had a head injury.

As someone from the lab exited the room, she entered. Standing at the head of the bed, she saw the man yank his arm away as one of the nurses tried to insert a large bore IV catheter into his arm. Taking out her pen light, Hannah checked his eyes. While a bit sluggish, they did react to the light. Noting the oval shape of one of his pupils, however, Hannah anticipated a major problem. The intracranial pressure in his head was building.

"What was his GCS?" she asked the nurse who was busy recording the patient's vitals. The Glasgow Coma Scale would give them a clearer understanding of the man's consciousness level. Anything within the range of three to eight, Hannah knew, meant the patient was comatose.

"It was a twelve on scene but just dropped to eight," he said, never taking his eyes off the monitors that displayed the patient's vital signs. "He needs to go to surgery now. It's up to those two as to who gets to take him first."

Hannah looked over to see that William had entered the room along with the trauma surgeon, Dr. Weeks.

"What did the CT show?" she asked as William joined her at the patient's bedside.

"He has a large subdural hematoma. The OR team is on its way now to take him for an exploratory. If Dr. Weeks can get the internal bleeding stopped and the patient makes it through the surgery, we'll go in and evacuate it," William said as he conducted his own assessment of the patient, checking his pupil response and then examining the head laceration.

"Is he stable enough for two surgeries?" Hannah asked, feeling helpless as she watched the patient deteriorate before her eyes. More than once as a nurse, she had wished for the surgical skills that would allow her to take a patient to the operating room herself instead of having to wait for the surgeon on call to show up.

"We don't have a choice. He needs a crani to decrease his intracranial pressure or he won't have a chance. We'll just have to hope that Dr. Weeks finds the bleeding and fixes it fast." William stepped away from the young man's bedside. "I'm going to go talk to his family."

Hannah looked up as one of the monitors beeped an alarm.

"What's the holdup? This guy needs surgery now," Dr. Weeks said as the OR team charged into the room. "Let's go before he codes."

Hannah followed the team out of the room and joined William in the hallway to accompany him to meet with the family. Having never been in a critical care waiting room before, she knew it usually meant a patient was near death.

The room was full of people, all in some form of grief. Everyone stopped when she and William entered, and Hannah could feel the weight of their stares. Their eyes said they were expecting the worse, their expressions revealed they were all full of hope. How did William handle this kind of responsibility?

"I'm Dr. Cooper," William announced. "I'm the neurosurgeon called in to see Kyle. I was told his wife was here."

The group seemed to part as a woman not quite Hannah's age stepped forward. "I'm his wife and this is Kyle's mother and father."

The young woman indicated the older couple beside her. "Is he...?" Her voice broke on the words.

"He's headed to the OR right now. As I'm sure Dr. Weeks told you, Kyle's condition is critical."

Hannah listened as William clarified some of the details of Kyle's surgery to decrease the cranial pressure. He used words the family would understand, explaining that the accumulation of blood was pushing on Kyle's brain and could cause permanent damage. She felt she had learned as much by listening to him than she had ever learned in one of those dry nursing school lectures halls. By the time he had received their consent to proceed with the neurosurgery, his phone was alerting him to a message.

"Dr. Weeks has located the source of the bleed," he told Kyle's family after reading the message. "As he suspected, it was the spleen. He's removing it now... I'm going to get ready. I'll have an OR nurse keep you up to date on our progress. I don't expect to be in surgery for very long," William added before he and Hannah headed out the door.

"Let me know when you finish. I'm going

to hang out in the employee lounge," she told him once they arrived at the door that led to the OR.

"I thought you'd want to come in with me," he said, swiping his ID badge to pass through the door.

"Really? You'll let me in the operating room with you?" she said. There had been a holdup with her paperwork from school and she hadn't yet been given hospital clearance to attend his surgeries.

"I got special permission from the medical chief for you to observe only. Come on, I'll show you where to change."

By the time Hannah was directed to an area off to William's side, where she wouldn't be in the surgical field but would still have a good view, she was starting experiencing some serious jitters. The smell of Betadine and blood mingled in the air as the surgical team prepared. She made herself concentrate on the way the technician draped Kyle's head for the procedure, her stomach continually rolling in protest. What if she couldn't take watching? Performing brain surgery had been her dream for years but she'd never actually been present for one.

Then William's soothing voice enveloped her as he explained each confident incision, the sound of soft classical music filling the room. Some surgeons liked hard rock in their ORs, others liked soft jazz. Hannah should have known he would go for Tchaikovsky.

Soon she had forgotten her fears and was totally caught up in the procedure as the blood that had accumulated underneath the skull was evacuated.

The anesthesiologist called out that the patient's blood pressure was dropping, but William's hands never faltered. His voice was always calm and steady, and it was easy to see why they called him the Ice Prince of the OR. He was able to separate himself from every emotion while he had a scalpel in his hand.

Hannah remembered wondering which of William's personas was the real one. She hadn't understood the nickname then. She'd needed to see him here, now, to fully appreciate where the ability to withdraw from everything happening around him gave him the power to save lives. Only, the real world wasn't like this sterile room. To really live, he had to open himself up to others instead of shutting them out.

And who was she to say anything about someone shutting others out? After everything she had been through with Lindsey's dad, and then her parents turning their backs on her, she'd shut herself in as much the same way as William had. Her fear of losing her daughter had taken control of every aspect of her life. She'd devoted herself to taking the best care of Lindsey. Yes, she'd made friends with other mothers and coworkers, but she hadn't let anyone inside her and Lindsey's world. Just as William hadn't let anyone inside his world until now.

Maybe it's time for me to make some changes in my life, too.

Hannah eyed the monitors and was relieved to see that the patient's blood pressure was starting to rise. The anesthesiologist called out the new reading.

As William prepared to close the incision, he explained that they would store the section of skull that had been removed until he could confidently replace it once Kyle's vitals and crania had time to restore themselves. Most assuredly, before the patient was sent to a rehab facility.

"Thank you," William said to the operating staff as he stepped back from the table. He then turned to Hannah. "Well, what do you think? Do you still want to specialize in neurosurgery?"

"Yes," she said as she replayed the operation over in her on head. She had no doubts now. She was meant to be in a neurosurgeon's practice. "This is definitely what I want to do."

CHAPTER SEVEN

WILLIAM STOPPED AT the bottom step of the house that had haunted his childhood. While his classmates had moaned about being sent off to boarding school, he had gladly left this place. Would things have been different if his father had sold the house after the accident? Would he have been different without the reminder every day of his mother's accident?

"This is where you grew up?" Lindsey asked from beside him.

"Yes," he answered without explaining that he had spent as much time away from the place as possible. Hannah's daughter had been raised in a home filled with love. He couldn't expect her to understand that his upbringing had been very different than hers.

"It would have been a cool place to play hide-and-seek when you were little. I bet you could hide for hours here," Lindsey said as she continued up the steps.

He'd spent most of his time hiding in his room or in the attic, but he didn't have many memories of anyone actually seeking him. As far as his stepmothers had been concerned, if he was out of sight, everything was fine. It was only when he'd showed up during one of their social functions that he'd become a problem. No one had been interested in the awkward child happier to be reading a book than talking with strangers.

The trip to Dallas had not been without challenges. While Lindsey had done her best to entertain Avery, the little girl had refused to be satisfied. She'd finally fussed herself to sleep. And that was why Hannah had insisted that they pack a bag to spend the night. She had known the trip there and back in one day would be more than any of them could handle.

He'd wanted to drive back to Houston that night, but he could now see that Hannah had known what she was talking about. A night trip would have been miserable for everyone. It was another lesson learned.

Lindsey had told him he should get a minivan with a DVD setup, but he drew the line at driving a "mommy van." That was not happening.

"It's a monstrosity that my father built to declare himself the king of Dallas real estate," he said as they climbed the steps to the front door. "'Real estate is all about perception,' he would say. 'No one wants to hire an unsuccessful agent.'"

"Are you okay?" Hannah asked, as she shifted Avery in her arms and reached for his hand.

Her touch was warm and comforting. Surprising himself, he closed his hand over hers. A strange calm came over him. Not like the calm that he demanded of himself in the OR, but a peaceful feeling that he wasn't alone. That there was someone to care enough to go through this with him. Was this friendship? Or was this something more? He should release Hannah's hand and step away, but at that moment he didn't know if he had the strength to go through the doors without her.

For the first time it really sank in that his father was gone. That he would never be there to greet William again. The weight of that knowledge slammed into him unexpectedly as he walked, hand in hand with Hannah, into the foyer where he had last seen the man.

He remembered taking a real good look at his father then—had acknowledged their similarities in height and coloring, and noted that his father's age had begun to show despite his fight to hold on to his youth.

His father had insisted that William come to meet his new wife. She'd turned out to be only a younger version of wife number three, whom he'd divorced a few years prior. William had made the effort; as always, hoping that he'd see some sign that his father had changed. There'd been no change. His newest stepmother had been surprisingly pleasant, though. An interior decorator before their marriage, she'd shared with him some of the changes she had planned for the house. But her time had run out too soon.

"Oh, there you are!" Ms. Adams, Avery's former nanny, called out as she rushed to Hannah's side and took Avery into her arms. "I've missed this one so much, but it's so nice to see that she's doing so well. And of course she belongs in Houston with her big brother, though I'm sure she's made a change or two in your life by now."

"This is Hannah. She's helping me and Avery with the transition," William said as he let go of Hannah's hand and immediately missed its warmth. "She would like to go through Avery's and her mother's things to see if there is anything we need to keep while I go through some of my father's paperwork.

"Would you also show her through the house, Mrs. Adams? I'll join you as soon as I'm finished," he added before leaving the women.

His father's lawyers had felt it necessary that he personally review some of the documents left in his father's private study. William had no idea what he was going to find, but would rather be buried in his father's paperwork than dealing with all the memories that he wasn't ready to face.

Hannah watched as William headed to a side door and disappeared.

If William's father had really wanted to impress, this was definitely the house for it. How in the world would Avery's mother have kept up with a toddler in a house this size? And, as far as she could see, there was nothing at all that looked child friendly,

She moved farther into the house, looking for anything that would tell her about the people who had lived there. She was hoping there would be something to explain William's outlook toward the house. Somehow, she knew that his whole attitude about family was tied to the childhood he had spent here.

After taking in the sitting room at the front of the house—Lindsey asking Mrs. Adams where they hid the television—they moved to a formal living room and dining room. Marble, wood, and crystal filled every room. Definitely impressive, but cold and impersonal, too. While Hannah was sure the rooms had been designed to impress, she struggled to grasp a sense of the people, the family, that had lived here not that long ago.

It wasn't until the former nanny finally took them upstairs to Avery's room that Hannah could see the small touches that made a place feel lived in. Before Ms. Adams could put her down, Avery was squealing for a ride on the toy train mounted on a set of rails that circled the room.

Lindsey helped her onto the seat and began to push her around the track while Avery laughed at the train sounds she was making.

The way those two had bonded was amazing. Lindsey had never asked for a sibling—somehow the child had known that their family would always be just the two of them.

A door stood open to a room done in pastel pinks and greens, the carpet as white as snow. "Was this Avery's parents' room?" Hannah asked as she stepped inside. A silver hairbrush lay on a dressing table that held bottles and jars with names of expensive products she had only seen advertised in elite fashion magazines.

"This was Mrs. Cooper's room. Mr. Cooper's room is down the hall," Mrs. Adams said. "Mrs. Cooper said her husband was a light sleeper and she was concerned that a baby would disturb him so she had this room decorated before Miss Avery was born."

Hannah could tell that the woman had more to say about her employee-employer relationship, but for now Hannah wanted to make her own observations. If there was something in this house that would explain why William was so withdrawn from other people, she didn't think she would find it in this room.

But there was something Ms. Adams could help her with.

"I was wondering if you knew where Avery's mother would have kept any photographs of Avery. You know, hospital photos, or her first time crawling? I know when she's older, she will want those. Also, anything special that you think we should keep for her. A favorite toy or book?" Hannah asked as she turned to the woman. "And anything of her mother's that she might appreciate later." She fingered the silver hairbrush. Had Avery's mother once used it to brush the child's dark curls?

"I helped the staff from the lawyers' office collect Mrs. Cooper's jewelry. They assured me it would be kept safe until Avery was old enough to keep it herself."

Mrs. Adams turned back to where Lindsey and Avery were playing in the room next door. "They only asked for the things they could put a dollar value to since they were cataloging those items." She took a hesitant breath. "No one seemed to really care about the little girl who had been left behind without her parents. I was so glad when the lawyers asked me to take her to her brother. She needed someone who wasn't looking at the dollar signs, it seemed to me."

The older woman smiled at Hannah before continuing. "I guess it took some time for the lawyers to find her parents' most recent will. But I had heard about Mr. Cooper's son being a doctor and all, and it made sense that the Coopers would want the child with her brother. The staff that had been here awhile spoke well of him, so it seemed to me that was where the child belonged. I wish you could have seen his eyes when I handed him little Avery."

Hannah stared at the woman with admiration. She was a lot feistier than her gray hair pulled back in a sedate knot at the back of her head and her feet clad in a pair of comfortable-looking sneakers made her appear. The woman was opinionated and certainly not afraid to tell you exactly what she thought.

"But I can tell he's doing better now," Mrs. Adams stated. "I knew from what I had heard of him that he wouldn't turn his back on his responsibilities. I'm so glad he found someone to help him with Avery."

"I'm just a friend, a coworker. We work together at the hospital," Hannah found herself telling the woman. It wasn't as if she needed to explain the arrangement to her.

A squeal came from the other room and they both rushed in to see Lindsey blowing raspberries against Avery's tummy, the child bubbling over with laughter.

"I'm so glad you are there for them." Mrs. Adams grinned at the children rolling on the floor. "Avery needed a real home and it looks like she's found one."

Hannah couldn't bring herself to tell Mrs. Adams that the family arrangement she was imagining for the little girl was just temporary.

It was becoming harder for her to believe that what she was feeling for both Avery and William wasn't real. Even Lindsey was forming a close connection with both Avery and William. The four of them fit too well together and she needed to remember that she was only there for a short time.

Soon, very soon, William wouldn't need her anymore and it would be time for her and Lindsey to move on. They'd moved on before. They could do it again.

Why hadn't she listened to William earlier when he'd told her it would be best for them to drive back to Houston than to spend the night in his father's house? She'd heard something in his voice at the time, but had chosen to ignore it.

Instead, she'd truly believed that having the night in her old home would be good for Avery. She'd also thought it would give her time to observe what items seemed most significant to the little girl. And that was why she now found herself trying to fall asleep in a dead woman's bed—where Hannah knew she didn't belong.

She'd been glad that William hadn't reminded her of his desire not to stay overnight. She'd even been surprised when he'd suggested ordering pizza and eating it in the small game room on the second floor where he had unearthed an old gaming system for him and Lindsey to play.

For a couple of hours, they had relaxed. Hannah playing on the floor with Avery while the other two screamed taunts of revenge at one another. It wasn't until after she had said good-night to William and seen Lindsey to the guest room, that the eerie feeling that she didn't belong in the room next to Avery's nursery had begun to haunt her.

It wasn't only the thought of Avery's mother spending her last night alive here, though it seemed sad that the woman had this big, beautiful room and still slept alone. It was the whole house. What had the late Mrs. Cooper seen when William's father had brought her here for the first time? Had she been impressed with all that wood and marble? Or had she found it cold and lifeless, like Hannah had? She couldn't imagine how William must have felt growing up in such a place. Or could she? Was the very nature of the mansion part of the explanation for William's aloofness?

Hannah punched the pillow and turned onto her side. She had no right judging the people who had lived here, but she couldn't help but compare this place to the home William had made. In some ways his house had seemed cold when she'd first entered it, but as she'd added small items and changed the grouping of some of the furniture, she had soon seen the possibilities in the house and it was quickly becoming a home for the four of them.

It's only temporary, she reminded herself. She heard the screech of metal against metal and froze. Surely it was her imagination? There were only the four of them in this wing of the house, so who would be up moving around at this time? The sound of a board squeaking had her up and at Avery's bedside in less than a minute. The child was safe in her crib and sound asleep. She took a moment to brush soft wisps of hair from Avery's face then headed to the door that opened into the hallway.

Had Lindsey woken and been disoriented as to where she was? Or, more likely, had her daughter decided to do some exploring on her own while the adults slept?

Stepping up to the guest room door, Hannah cracked it open. Her daughter was stretched out in sleep as if she didn't have a care in the world, something that always made Hannah smile. Like every transplant recipient family, they knew that their lives could change at any moment, but Hannah didn't allow either one of them to spend time worrying about what the future could hold. They'd face that together when the time came.

Having assured herself that both Avery and Lindsey were where they should be, she headed along the hall to the room William had chosen for the night and stopped. What was she thinking? She couldn't just barge into the man's room! But even knowing the girls were safe wasn't enough. She needed to make sure that William was okay, too.

Rounding the corner, she saw that his bedroom door was open. Seeing his empty bed—a sight that had her body humming with dangerous excitement—she considered what to do next. It only made sense that the sounds she had heard were William's. The man had the right to prowl the halls of his father's home at night if he wanted to. But still, there would be no going to sleep for her until she could assure herself that he was okay. Had he been feeling the same out-of-sorts sensations she had? Just being in this house had to be hard so soon after the loss of his father. Of course, it could be that William wanted to be alone with his thoughts, but it seemed to her that he had been alone too much already in his life.

Her mind made up, Hannah headed for the stairs. She would check on William then leave him alone if he wished. She just needed to see him and, no matter what other parts of her body seemed to think, she was just checking to make sure he didn't need anything.

Like a friendly hug? she asked herself.

The kitchen was empty, but the light over the back stairway was on. She wasn't sure where it led, but she was certain she'd find William there.

Opening the fridge, she pulled out some milk and then checked the cabinets for the makings of hot cocoa. The warm, sweet beverage had always worked to calm her nerves, which was something she could use now as she contemplated following William up those stairs.

CHAPTER EIGHT

WILLIAM STOOD AMONG the boxes and furniture relegated to the attic when their usefulness ended. Somewhere in here, there was a box of his mother's belongings. Things his father had ordered removed from their bedroom when it had been determined that his wife would never be returning. But that wasn't what William was after.

He'd been through that box many times as a child missing his mother. Anything he'd thought needed to be preserved, he had removed and snuck back to the box he'd kept under his bed. The box that he had later hidden in the attic when he'd left for college. The box he had all but forgotten about until he'd planned this trip to gather some of Avery's mother's belongings.

He should have thought of that himself.

The few things he'd had of his mother's had been priceless as he'd grown up and time had started to erase his memories. He didn't want that for Avery. He'd make sure that she always had access to her mother's belongings. William wouldn't be like his father and hide everything away. He'd even taken the picture he'd found in the office of their father holding Avery as an infant. He planned to place it on the fireplace mantel in his home.

Going over his father's accounts today, he had made the decision to sell the house and put all the proceeds into a trust fund for Avery that his father had already set up.

He only wanted one thing from this house and he needed to find it before they left in the morning. This would be his final trip to his father's ostentatious estate. He would leave everything else for the lawyers to handle.

"Here you are," Hannah said, her head peaking over the railing of the attic stairs.

He turned and watched as she stepped onto the landing, holding two cups. He enjoyed the sight of her tousled blond waves and the thin nightshirt that hugged her curves.

"What are you doing here?" he asked as

he took one of the cups and a big step back from her.

"I heard something in the hall and saw that your bed was empty. I wanted to make sure you were okay," Hannah said.

"You checked my bed?" he asked, amused when a light pink blush stained her cheeks.

"I checked on Avery and Lindsey first," she said, looking around the large space. "I know it's your house, but everything I've learned from watching horror movies with Lindsey tells me that coming up into the attic at night is not a good move."

"But you came anyhow?" he asked, setting down his cup.

"My parents always said my curiosity would get me in trouble someday." She gave him a smile then turned to lift a sheet off the old desk that had been in storage since he'd been a little boy.

Did she not realize that he was the trouble her parents had warned her about?

"Are you looking for something particular?" she asked.

He'd come to the attic to be alone with his memories, but now he wanted to share those memories with Hannah. He wanted to let her see the lonely boy that had grown up to be the man he was today. The man whose coworkers referred to him as Dr. Frosty. Was it weak to want Hannah to understand him? Did he care if it was? He found himself wanting to share more and more with her every day. He'd waited for the fear of rejection to come, but it hadn't. He trusted Hannah, something he'd once thought impossible.

"That desk was my mother's," he said, shuffling boxes in the far corner of the room where he'd hidden his most prized possessions.

"It's lovely. You must miss her," she said, her voice coming from directly behind him.

He'd known she'd ask questions; her curiosity was something he enjoyed. He'd seen it in her interest in everything about their work, about Avery, about everyone and everything. Someone else might call her snoopy, but he had come to understand that it was just her desire to learn. To know those around her.

Moving a large box marked "Christmas," he paused then said, "I do. It's not something I speak of very often, though."

He indicated a low bench under the eaves of the attic where a window looked out against the dark sky. "Let's sit over there," he said, picking up a small black box with the words "Private Letters" painted along the side in dark red paint.

William waited for Hannah to begin with her questions, but they didn't come. Taking a seat beside her on the bench, he looked out across a yard that held a lifetime of memories for him. Only, for his mother. it had been a very short lifetime.

"I was nine when Bennie, a man who worked for my father's business, came to get me from school. I had been expecting my mother as she was usually the one who picked me up. I didn't think much of it until I realized Bennie wasn't driving me home. He tried to explain to me that there had been an accident. My mother had fallen and hit her head and was very sick, but the only thing I understood was that my mother was in the hospital."

William would never forget the first time he had seen his mother in the hospital bed, tubes and monitors surrounding her. He'd not understood why she wouldn't wake up when he'd called her name. Day after day, he had gone to see the woman lying in that bed, her head wrapped in dressings. And day after day, he'd become angrier and angrier with her for not waking. For not coming back to him.

"It wasn't until later, after my father explained that my mother would be going to a place that could take better care of her than the hospital, that I realized she was never coming home." He took a deep breath.

"I'm sorry. That must have been terrible," Hannah sympathized.

"Yes. She suffered a traumatic brain injury when she fell and, despite all the specialists my father sent to see her, there was never any hope of recovery." He paused. "She passed away five years ago."

"That's why you went into neurosurgery," she said.

"I used to tell her every time I saw her that someday I'd be a doctor and I'd make her well. If I had known then what I know now, I would have made my father let her go when they first put her on a ventilator," he said.

"Thank you for sharing that with me. I know it can't be easy for you to come here with the memories of your mother and now your father."

"We weren't that close, my father and I.

I think that maybe we were just too much alike in some ways. We were always bumping heads over something—most of the time it wasn't even anything important. Something happened when we lost my mother and we just never could work things out between us. I won't let things be like that for me and Avery. I won't let that history be repeated," he said as he opened the top of the black box and pulled out a handmade card.

"What's that?" she asked, leaning over. "Oh, a Mother's Day card. I have a box of them that Lindsey's made for me."

"It was the last one I made for my mother," he said then set it aside. She didn't need to know how angry his father had become when William had insisted on taking the card to his mother. It was the same day his father had rasped through gritted teeth that his mother would never be able to read the card. Would never be able to come home again.

Hannah reached into the box and brought out a signed baseball. "Astros?"

"Rangers. My father's company sponsored a family fun night when I was eleven," William said.

He let her examine the strange collection

that had come from his childhood. An old picture of Elle Campbell from the eighth-grade dance. A rock from a riverbed he'd collected on the trip he had taken with his grandparents to the mountains of Tennessee.

Hannah held up an empty perfume bottle. It had been his mother's, one of the few things he had taken from the boxed items the staff had put it the attic. Over the years, the fragrance had evaporated until only the empty bottle remained. Just as his hope that his mother would return for him had dried up as the weeks and months had stretched into years.

"I had forgotten about these things until you mentioned gathering things for Avery," he said, gently taking the bottle from her and holding it to the light of the bulb hanging above them. "You were right, Hannah. There are things of her mother's that Avery will treasure when she gets older. You always seem to know the right thing to do."

"Me? I wish," she said and then hesitated.

He waited and watched as she bit down on her lower lip. A warm heat spread through him, part desire and part something else... something he refused to acknowledge.

"I've made a lot of mistakes," she finally said. "Done the wrong thing. Said the wrong thing. They've taught me some hard lessons."

"Was one of those mistakes Lindsey's father?" he asked, his curiosity getting the better of him.

"Best mistake I ever made," Hannah breathed. "It gave me Lindsey. She's a blessing, not a mistake. It was her father who was the mistake."

"I didn't mean Lindsey," he said. The funny girl who kept him on his toes was delightful.

"I know you didn't. But yes, in other ways, my relationship with Lindsey's father was a mistake."

"I take it he's not involved with Lindsey?" he asked. Did the man know what he was missing? Any man would be proud to be the girl's father.

"No. He had plans for his life that didn't include me or a baby. By the time I figured out that I was just a rebound relationship for him, he'd gotten back with his high school sweetheart."

"It's his loss, you know," William said as he put his cherished items back inside the box. "And I'm not just talking about Lindsey."

"Thank you," Hannah said. "I know it would have been easier if I'd had help, but it wasn't meant to be. Me and Lindsey—we were meant to be."

"Your parents couldn't help?" he asked. He knew from conversations he'd overheard between Hannah and her daughter that things were very tense between Hannah and her parents.

"That's a story for another time... It's going to be a long car ride back to Houston tomorrow. We'd both better get some sleep."

Putting the lid back on the box, he stood, stashed it under one arm, and reached out a hand to help Hannah up from the bench.

For a mere second, they stood together, hands linked, bodies all but touching, breaths mingling.

William felt more aroused then he had ever felt in his life but he took a step back. This couldn't happen. Not here in this house. Not now. Because as much as he had tried to warn Hannah against him, deep inside he knew that no matter the risk, someday soon he would not be able to walk away from the hunger in her eyes.

"I'm not the man you think I am, Hannah."

He tensed when she stepped closer to him, fought his body's arousal.

Resting her hands against his chest, she lifted her lips to his in a soft caress.

"You're not the man you think you are, either," she said before turning away, leaving him wondering what was it that she saw in him given all the baggage he carried with him.

CHAPTER NINE

LEAVING THE OPERATING ROOM, Hannah all but danced. She had passed the test required by the hospital to allow her to assist William in the OR and she couldn't wait to get back to the office to tell him. Her phone vibrated in the back pocket of her scrub pants and she pulled it out to see a text from William asking how it was going.

Done and passed! she typed. Her phone rang immediately.

"Meet me in the emergency room," William said, his words clipped, cold. She knew the tone only too well now. There was a critical patient who was not doing well.

"I'll head there now," she said as a bit of the adrenaline from her excitement drained from her.

While she understood why William internalized his feelings during surgery and when dealing with a patient that needed emergency care, she wondered how healthy it was for him to hold it all inside. It seemed that underneath all that control lay the root of whatever it was that made him think he needed to go through his life alone.

She'd only recently realized that even all of his hobbies were solitary. Had he spent so much time alone in the house his father had built that he didn't know how to live life any other way? Of course, his life was changing now with Avery. Whether within his comfort zone or not, he would be joining the rest of the world.

She spotted William's tall frame and brown hair above a group standing outside one of the trauma rooms and joined them. She also spotted a couple of officers, which sent shivers through her. Their presence meant that the patient was likely either a crime victim or a suspect.

"Excuse me," she said as she pushed past an X-ray technician leaving the crowded space.

Then she saw her.

Her arm still wrapped in the Velcro splint

she'd been wearing the last time Hannah had seen her, there was now an ugly scar above her eye, the greenish hue of old bruises standing out against her pale face.

Jeannine Jones had been intubated and a respiratory tech was quickly setting up the ventilator. Grabbing a pair of gloves from the dispenser, Hannah made it to the side of Jeannine's bed. She carefully pushed the woman's hair back from the side of her face to assess her swollen, bloody eye.

"Orbital fracture?" she asked as William joined her.

"No, thank God. The blow knocked her back and she hit her head against a fireplace hearth. CT shows a cranial fracture with a subdural hematoma that I'll have to fix in the OR once she's stabilized."

He showed no emotion to the outside world, but Hannah knew him now and he didn't have to raise his voice for her to see how angry he was that they hadn't been able to save this woman. Did he look at her lying so lifelessly and see the body of his mother? she wondered.

"Where's her husband?" Hannah asked the

officer taking information from the emergency doctor.

"He's in custody. The neighbor called us when she heard him shouting at her. We found Mrs. Jones on the floor, him passed out drunk beside her," the officer said.

The monitor beeped as Jeannine's heart rate climbed.

"Are you going to be okay assisting?" William asked Hannah. There was no censure in his words, no judgment if she refused. Hadn't that been just what she had been doing to him earlier? Judging him by his emotional reactions?

There was emotion in the man. He wasn't the Ice Prince everyone saw in the OR. She'd seen him laughing as he'd played on the floor with his sister just last night. It was easy to see the love he felt for Avery. And he was working hard to be the parent he needed to be for her.

Hannah looked down at Jeannine, whom she had only met once but had worried about often, imagining her being mistreated by her husband. This was what she'd always dreamed of doing. Though her part was only to follow William's directions, it was still close enough to make her heart race. She wiped her gloved palms against her pants. She had to take this step now to prove herself. Not just to William, but to herself.

"If you take her to surgery, I'm going with you." she said. "Was there anything else we could have done to help her?"

"I don't know. I spoke to the neuro social worker who met with her the last time she was here. Staff had tried to talk Jeannine out of leaving with Calvin, but she wouldn't listen. In the end, our hands were tied. Not that it makes me feel any better," William said as he left the room. "I'll have you paged if we're going to the OR."

While Hannah waited to hear if they would be taking Jeannine to the OR, she made a trip to the cafeteria. The last thing she needed was to be weak in the OR and embarrass herself.

"Hannah?" a soft voice inquired.

She turned to find a beautiful, dark-haired woman standing behind her—with a baby bump she couldn't mistake. "Sarah, you're pregnant!"

"I know. And thank you for not adding *again*."

"You look beautiful. I can't believe I didn't know," Hannah said—and meant it.

With Lindsey carpooling to her riding lessons, Hannah hadn't seen Sarah in weeks. She made a mental note to herself that once her studying was done, she would take some time to see her friends. She'd missed Sarah. The nurse practitioner who had played such a big part in Lindsey and Hannah's lives by advocating for the transplant was beautiful both inside and out. Even after Lindsey's surgery, she had been there to advise Hannah throughout nursing school.

"Lindsey tells me you've almost finished with your practitioner classes," Sarah said, following Hannah to the cashier. They each took their turn swiping their payment and found a table where they could catch up.

"I'm so close right now. I've got my preceptor hours with Dr. Cooper and I've learned so much," Hannah said.

"According to Lindsey, there's more than learning going on between you and William Cooper. I hear you've moved in together."

Oh, no. What had Lindsey been telling people?

"It's not like it sounds. I mean…yes, Lindsey and I are living with him. But it's only a temporary arrangement. He just needed some…help and it works out better if we live together." Hannah tried to clarify, saying, "It's more like an exchange of information."

"Maybe you need to start from the beginning," Sarah said as she sat her coffee cup down, "because somehow I have a feeling this is going to get complicated."

Hannah did as she asked, telling Sarah how William had come to have custody of his baby sister and had needed some guidance on the day-to-day care of a soon-to-be toddler. She explained that she had been given a chance to work with the neurosurgeon and also get her educational hours in while having evenings off with Avery and Lindsey.

"I have to say I'm a little disappointed," Sarah said as she pushed her tray away.

"I don't understand," Hannah replied. She thought a lot of the woman who had made such a difference in her daughter's life. Without Sarah's advocating so hard for Lindsey's transplant, it might not ever have happened. Sarah's example had been what had helped Hannah make the decision to go to nursing school. She would never want to disappoint her.

"I was hoping that maybe you'd finally taken some time for yourself. Some time for romance, Hannah. And I can't imagine anyone being more perfect for you than William."

"You know that's not what I want. My biggest responsibility is to Lindsey right now. The last thing I need is a man in my life," Hannah scoffed.

"You have noticed that William's a man, haven't you? And he is in your life, right? From what Lindsey says, y'all are getting along great," Sarah said.

Hannah hated to admit that Sarah was right. There was no doubt that William was a man—she was more aware of that than she should be. And Lindsey was right, too. Somehow the four of them living together worked.

It surprised her, now that she thought about it, but they had both been two single people living alone—except for Lindsey, of course— and they'd been happy with their lifestyles. If someone had asked if she would be agreeable to living with someone else, Hannah would have said no. She was too used to living independently to deal with someone else in her space and she was pretty sure William felt the same way.

But the two of them had worked through all those awkward problems that came with sharing a home. And, for the most part, things were working well. They had each made concessions and were happy with the current arrangement.

No, she admitted, she was more than happy with what the two of them shared now. But what about William? Was she just a means to an end for him? He'd made it more than plain that he'd liked his life before Avery had come to live with him. But he had made so many changes since then. He was really working hard to be the best substitute parent for Avery that he could be. But it wasn't all about Avery.

The hours they spent together at night after the kids had gone to bed had become one of her favorite times of the day. They shared experiences with each other, talking not only about the job and the kids, but about themselves. He told her about things he had seen that he thought would be of interest to her. She told him about something she had read that might interest him. Things had begun to change between the two of them. They'd become friends...and maybe even more.

"Hannah?" Sarah asked.

Hannah realized her friend was staring at her as if she had lost her mind. She also realized there was a good possibility that she had lost not only her mind but also her heart.

"So, I was right. There is more than you're telling me," Sarah said, briefly covering Hannah's left hand with hers. "Look, I've known William for a while now, and he's a good man."

"You have?" Hannah asked. For someone who said he wanted to be left on his own, he did seem to know a lot of people.

"I have. He's a big donor for our therapy program at the ranch. He covers the cost of all the safety equipment we use, including all the helmets we give each student," Sarah told her. "I've also heard he donates a lot of money to the children's oncology department. And everyone knows what a good surgeon he is and how good he is with his patients.

"It's not something he wants attention for," Sarah attested. "That's not why he does it. He cares about people. I just don't think he's had that many people in his life who have cared about him. Which brings us back to you…" Sarah paused. "Hannah, I know you pretty well, too. You can't help but get involved with people—your patients, your classmates—you care for everyone. Sometimes that can put you at a disadvantage. I don't want to see you get hurt."

"I know I'm out of my league with William," Hannah said, giving up on getting the soup down and pushing her tray aside.

"No. From what you've told me, I'd say he's out of your league. I've seen the women he dates. They all look like the dolls we use to play with as kids—beautiful to look at but only fluff cotton inside. Not one of them would have done what you've done for him. You have to be scaring the life out of him, and I think that's a good thing. Emotions are messy and sometimes uncontrollable, which is not something William's had a lot of experience with."

Sarah was seeing romance, Hannah thought to herself, when, in reality, what William and Hannah had was a good friendship. And that was all it could ever be.

Her phone pinged with a message from William. They were going to the OR. With a hug and a thank you to Sarah, she headed off to get ready, pushing thoughts of what Sarah had said out of her mind.

William's hand was steady as he made the first cut, his mind fighting the doubts he still had about Jeannine Jones's outcome. Still, if she was going to have a chance at any quality of life, he knew he had to do whatever he could.

He took the procedure one precise step at a time, Hannah beside him, anticipating his needs for irrigation and suction. By the time he'd elevated the cranial bone and noted the blood flow increase, they had fallen into a natural complementary rhythm.

"Her blood pressure is dropping and her heart rate is up," the anesthesiologist announced. "Do we have any more trauma blood?"

"Cautery," William said to the OR tech, his hand out for the instrument. "Hannah, can you adjust the light?" He took care of the bleeders, concentrating on each detail as he ignored the others working around him.

"How's she doing?" he asked the anesthesiologist.

"Hypotensive, but starting to level off," she answered.

He evacuated a large clot and cauterized another section before preparing to close, repairing tears as he went. It was slow and tedious work but it had to be done.

"Heart rate one-fifty. Blood pressure beginning to drop again," the anesthesiologist informed him.

"Almost finished," William said as he began the work of reconstructing bone fragments. "I just need a few more minutes."

"Hang on, Jeannine," he heard Hannah say when the anesthesiologist called out for more blood. "Just hang on."

CHAPTER TEN

WILLIAM STARED BLANKLY at the computer screen in front of him. He'd made the excuse of wanting to catch up on some charting when he had sent Hannah home earlier. That had been hours ago. Since then, he'd haunted the recovery room to check on Jeannine Jones's blood pressure and consulted with a couple of new patients.

Back in the Neuro Critical Care Unit, just staring into space, it wouldn't take a psych doctor to tell him he had a problem. In fact, he could probably write a whole book on his emotional defects. Mommy issues. Daddy issues. He could see all of them in himself.

Until now, William had never minded his limitations. He had come to see that his shortcomings had helped make him the doctor he was today. The fact that he could isolate himself from everything around him while operating, including any feelings he might have for his charge, afforded him an innate ability to concentrate all his skills on his patient.

But that did not explain why he was sitting vigil for a patient he had only met once. Except, perhaps, for those mommy issues. Issues that made him fear that by saving Jeannine' life, he might be sentencing her to the fate of his own mother. If he saved Jeannine's life but she spent her last years comatose, he would have failed her. She had been a prisoner in her home with her husband; he couldn't bear to think of her as a prisoner in her own body.

"Hey, Dr. Cooper, how's it going?" asked one of the more seasoned nurses working the NCCU.

"Hey, Tom. You taking care of Mrs. Jones tonight?" William asked, turning his eyes from the computer screen. He'd reviewed every note that had been made on Jeannine's visits to the hospital and he couldn't find anything that might have changed the outcome. There was a paper trail a mile long detailing the escalation of her husband's violence, but the woman had denied it every time, leaving their hands tied.

"Yeah, I got her. Why don't you go on home? I'll call if something changes," Tom said, taking the seat next to William. "It's wrong what her husband did to her. So wrong. In my way of thinking, he can't be much of a man if he beats on his wife. The woman doesn't weigh a hundred pounds and she's barely over five feet tall."

"Yeah, I agree with you. It seems that love has struck again," William said, hearing the bitterness in his voice but not caring.

"That ain't love. We both know that. Love can make you do a lot of crazy things, but beating up on the person you love? No, that's nothing like love."

Changing the subject, Tom said, "Hey, I saw Hannah at the grocery store with Lindsey and the cute little girl she said was your half sister. That's crazy, man, right?"

"Yes, it's been pretty crazy." William looked down at his watch. Avery would be asleep by now. If someone had told him a month ago that he'd be upset because he'd missed reading a bedtime story to an eleventh-month-old, he would have thought them crazy. Now, he spent all day looking forward to getting home in time to put Avery to bed and to make sure Lindsey didn't need his help with her homework. And then, finally, when the house was nice and quiet, to enjoying a glass of wine with Hannah as they caught up with each other's day.

"I know I've never seen Hannah so happy and, after everything she's been through with her own little girl, it's nice. It's real nice. Now that is love for you," the RN said. One of the monitors beside them began to beep. "Gotta check that," Tom said, "but like I said, you go on home. I'll call if anything changes on Mrs. Jones."

Was Tom saying that Hannah was in love? No. He'd been talking about her love for Lindsey. Anyone who saw the two of them together knew that Hannah loved her daughter.

Rubbing his eyes, William stood and stretched. He knew that Tom was right, like always. He needed to go home and get some sleep. If he was lucky, he'd get in six hours before Avery woke and he had to start his day again.

* * *

Hannah filled her wineglass then settled on the couch where she was trying to finish a paper on community healthcare before the weekend. They had planned a party for Avery's first birthday, along with a trip to the zoo, and she didn't want to have to worry about homework then.

Unfortunately, she couldn't concentrate on the words she needed to finish it. It had only taken one evening without William being there for her to realize how much she missed him. No matter how much she had denied her feelings to Sarah and to herself, what Hannah felt for William was stronger than any friendship she had ever had before. Was it love? How would she know? The one time she had thought she was in love had been a mistake.

If she could just forget the feel of William against her back that night in the gym and the touch of his lips when she'd kissed him in the attic. He'd been right when he'd said she didn't know the rules to playing games with men. The only game she knew was how to play it safe. She had learned the hard way not to trust other people.

Only, something had changed that night in

the attic. He had trusted her with his child-hood memories. She'd seen the hurt little boy whose life had been torn apart when his mother had been taken away from him. Having her still alive for all those years, but not with him, had probably made things even worse for the young boy; he'd always hoped that she would return to him.

But those were the emotions of a child. Somewhere along the way to adulthood, William had decided to leave behind all his childhood attachments. Did he see himself as weak because of the hurt and pain he'd felt at losing his mother? Or had it been his father's example—packing up William's mother's belongings and relegating them to the cold, dark attic, as if boxing away all the love and pain meant it no longer existed?

Hannah had no right to judge William's father too harshly. She had never met the man and she knew things weren't always as they seemed.

As a child, she'd thought she would always be able to trust her parents' love. Then she'd grown up and realized that their love was dependent on her following what they thought was best for her life, instead of supporting her when she had needed them the most.

Even now, she refused to depend on anyone else. She'd separated herself from anyone wanting control over her and had devoted her life to her daughter. She'd only allowed herself to be surrounded by those she knew couldn't hurt her. She'd locked away her heart just as William had, and she hadn't even realized it. Until now. Because it wasn't just his body and his friendship that she wanted. She wanted it all. But that wasn't in either of their plans.

She stood, sloshing her wine onto the floor. Setting the glass on a side table, she grabbed a rag from the bar, wiped up the spill then deposited the rag in the sink. Unable to sit still another minute, she walked over to the window and stared out at the reflection of the moon against the backyard.

"Hannah?" She heard the voice behind her and turned. William's face seemed drained of color, his eyes heavy from lack of sleep.

"How's Jeannine?" Hannah asked as she moved to him. She wanted to open her arms and have him step into them. She wanted to take away the pain she knew he still carried from his childhood. She wanted to be able to fix whatever it was that was broken inside him. She wanted to make him feel all the emotions that locked inside him.

"There's no change. They'll call if they need me. You should be sleeping," he said as he removed his jacket and undid his tie before running his hand through his hair. Never had he looked more human, more approachable, than at that moment.

Hannah pushed his hands away from the top button of the shirt he had been fighting to open.

"What are you doing?" he asked, his voice a low growl that vibrated against her hands and sent her blood racing.

How could she explain the loneliness she had felt sitting there waiting for him? How missing him tonight had become a pain in her chest? How could she explain what she was feeling when she didn't understand it herself? Could he feel how much she needed him right then? How much she wanted him to take her in his arms and hold her close? Could she make him as desperate for her touch as she was for his? She opened one button and then the next before resting her hands against his chest to support legs that had suddenly gone weak.

"Talk to me, Hannah," William said, his body tensing beneath her hands.

"Tell me what you're feeling right now," she said, moving her hands higher to rest on his shoulders.

"You don't want to play games with me," he said as his arms came around her.

"I thought you liked to play games. Do you want me to go first?" She shifted until their bodies pressed together and she could feel him hard against her abdomen. She released the breath she had been holding as she'd waited for him to push her away. Stretching her body against his till her hand tangled in his hair, Hannah cradled him against her pelvis.

"I want you to tell me exactly how much of that wine bottle you've drunk," he said. While he made no advances, neither did he pull away from her.

"I've only had half a glass. I'm not drunk, William." Looking into his eyes, she could see that he doubted her words. "Do I need to walk a straight line to prove it?"

She realized what he was doing, but it

wouldn't work. He could think of as many explanations for her behavior as he wanted, it still wouldn't change the fact that he was responding to her.

"Hannah, I don't want to hurt you," William said, though she noticed he still didn't move away. He wanted her, he just wasn't happy about it.

"The only thing I want right now is you, William, nothing else. If this isn't what you want then that's okay, but don't walk away because of some misguided fear that I don't know what I'm doing."

Hannah knew exactly what she was doing and she refused to regret one minute of it. All she wanted was for him to feel the same desperate desire that had overtaken her the minute she'd touched him. The same ache that flooded her senses with a need she had ignored for too long. But first, she needed to hear him say it, because she didn't want to spend the night with the man she knew had taken many others to his bed. She wanted the man who had stood in the attic and told her his deepest secrets. The man she had fallen a little bit in love with that very night.

She moved against him. He stiffened, his

body rigid with a control she was determined to break. Pulling his head to hers until his lips were just a breath away from hers, she whispered, "Tell me what you feel right now, William. Tell me what it is you feel when I touch you. Tell me what you need."

"You," he said as she brushed her chest against him, her nipples hardening into tight peaks against the cotton of her shirt. "I need you."

William released the hold he'd kept for so long and reached for what he wanted most. His lips crushed hers and his tongue fought for entrance. She wanted to know what he was feeling? He felt like he would explode if he didn't get inside her. He was hard and thick, and he fit perfectly against the soft curve of her belly. She wanted to know what he needed? By the time the night was up she'd know the feel of him against her, inside her, surrounding her, until this need that had eaten at him for weeks was erased. She thought she could play games with the cold bastard he was and not get burned? He knew better. She'd hate him when she realized that this was all the emotion he was capable of, that this was all he could give her, but it was too late for either of them to turn back now.

Hannah moaned against his mouth as he ground himself against her. Then she nipped at his tongue and he pulled back. "The kids," she said as she started on his shirt buttons, yelping as he flipped her over his shoulder and headed to his bedroom.

He pushed the door open without putting her down then he let her fall against the mattress. He couldn't help but smile when she laughed at his caveman antics before pulling him to her. He found himself laughing with her as they discarded the clothing that separated them.

Then he was inside her with one thrust. Their hands searched and their legs tangled. She moaned into his mouth and he felt pleasure vibrate through him. The strength of her innocent abandonment tore at something deep inside him. Something William fought to hold back from her, but she wouldn't let him. Wrapping her legs around his hips, Hannah took him deeper until he let go and gave her everything he had. She covered his face with kisses, muffling a scream as her body took all of him and he lost himself inside her.

As William drifted off to sleep in her arms, he realized that Hannah had been the one surrounding him for all this time.

CHAPTER ELEVEN

HANNAH WAITED AT the entrance to the zoo while Lindsey entertained herself and Avery by pushing the stroller back and forth. William had left that morning before she'd awakened, leaving only a text message that he would meet them by noon.

Before leaving the house this morning, she had called to check on Jeannine Jones. Her nurse had informed her that Dr. Cooper had already been in to see her and there had been no changes overnight.

A part of Hannah felt vulnerable after the night they had spent together. She didn't regret it. She'd never forget it. But in the early morning, she had realized that either last night would be the end of the relationship they had shared or it would make it stronger now that they had acknowledged their mutual attraction. Either way, things were going to change and William had already said that he didn't like change.

A silver sedan, top lowered, swept around the corner and pulled into a parking spot. Hannah let out a breath. She'd planned the day carefully so that Avery and William's first trip to the zoo would be a great experience.

"Hey," he said as he jogged up to them.

"Hey," she said, the heat of a blush climbing up her face. She had known this was going to be awkward. She had expected it. What surprised her, though, was the sharp flash of desire that struck her midsection and made her catch her breath. It was a need inside her that had her standing dumbstruck in its intensity. She had never felt anything like it before. For a second, Hannah understood William's desire to keep everyone at bay. This man could break her in two. Her brain warned her to protect her heart while her heart told her it was already too late.

"Mom? Will? Hello, you two?" Lindsey said, pushing the stroller between Hannah and William. "Y'all can stare at each other later. Me and Avery are ready to see some lions," Lindsey roared at Avery, sending the toddler off into giggles.

"Okay, then. Let's go," William said as he broke the connection that had ensnared them both. To her surprise, he took her hand in his.

"Lindsey, slow down," she said, catching up with the two.

Once inside, they meandered the paths, Lindsey leading the way.

"She knows her way around here pretty well, doesn't she," William observed.

"There wasn't a lot we could do together before she had her transplant. Most things were either too strenuous or too expensive. So we spent a lot of time visiting the zoo," she said.

"You don't talk a lot about it. Her heart transplant," he said as they paused to watch the pale pink flamingos flap their wings.

"The transplant was the easy part. It was the waiting for the transplant that was hard. The time she spent in the critical care unit of the hospital, knowing that time was running out and there was nothing I could do to help? That was the hard part, the part I know I might have to relive someday. That's why we don't talk about it. You learn to take each day as it comes when you don't know how many you have left."

"You're a strong woman, Hannah," William said admiringly as they left the flamingo exhibit to follow the kids down the next path.

They both watched as Lindsey made faces at the lemurs, Avery clapping her hands at the monkeys jumping from tree to tree. Instead of things being awkward between the two of them, Hannah and William fell into the comfort of a friendship that, while new, seemed much older. It was as if they had known one another for years, but were still learning a lot about each other.

"Have you heard anything from Avery's great-aunt?" she asked.

"I got an email from her saying she'd be in town in the next two weeks. I'm kind of nervous about it, too. I spoke with one of my father's estate lawyers. It seems that being Alison, Avery's mother's next of kin, she could take me to court for custody. It doesn't mean she would get it, but I don't want to take that chance."

There had been a time when Hannah had worried that the woman would show up. That she'd push the point that William was not prepared to care for a child Avery's age. But not any longer. William had worked hard, with a dedication that had been surprising. He could not be any more involved in Avery's care than if he had been her real father. She understood why the possibility of losing Avery worried him.

They tried to catch up with Lindsey as she sped away with Avery. "Lindsey, slow down."

"I'm fine, Mom," her daughter said, a big helping of preteen exasperation thrown in.

"She's in such a hurry to experience everything, as though she could make up for all those years she missed, that sometimes she does overdo it," Hannah told William.

"How about we let Avery out of the stroller for a while?" she asked Lindsey when they finally caught up. Bending to unbuckle the toddler, she added, "She needs her diaper changed, and that way you can go explore on your own. Do you have your phone?"

"Of course." Lindsey pulled it from her pocket and showed it to both adults.

"How about you meet us back at the small cat exhibit? Thirty minutes?" Hannah asked as she checked Avery and found her bottom dry.

"Okay! But I want to be there when Avery sees the big cats. She's going to love the lions." Lindsey rushed off, leaving the stroller with them.

"You don't think the lions will give her bad dreams or anything, do you?" William asked Hannah.

"She'll be fine. Bend down," she said as she lifted Avery and placed her on William's shoulders.

"Is she okay up there?" William stood frozen in place, his hands gripping the toddler's chubby legs. "She won't fall?" he asked as Avery laughed and rocked back and forth as if sitting on the glittery pink rocking horse they'd brought back from Dallas.

"Just hold on to her legs and she'll be fine."

They walked through the exhibits with first Hannah and then William reading the information out loud on each animal. By the time they made it to the giraffes, William had relaxed and both he and Avery were laughing as the long tongue of one of the giraffes lapped at the food pellets he held out in one hand. Hannah quickly pulled her phone and took a picture. She'd have it printed later and take it into William's office for his desk.

"Do you want to talk about it?" William asked as he yanked a sanitary wipe from Avery's bag and reached up to clean her small, chubby hands.

There was only one thing he could be talking about. Did she? So far, today had been wonderful, and Hannah didn't want to risk ruining it.

But wasn't that exactly what had happened with Lindsey's father? She'd avoided all conversations with him about their relationship because, deep down, she'd known she cared more for him than he cared for her. And now she had the same feeling again. William had made it clear that he had no plans to enter into a permanent relationship with anyone. That had changed somewhat with his custody of Avery, but that didn't mean anything else had changed.

This thing between the two of them was so new. Hannah didn't even know whether she wanted anything more than what they had right now. Couldn't they just enjoy the time they had together? No expectations. No worries. Just the two of them getting to know each other.

The beat of her heart slowed to a comfortable level. She was not repeating old mistakes, she told herself. Instead, she was opening herself up to new possibilities and hoping that William would follow her wherever it led them. Was that too much to ask?

"I'm not sure what it is we need to talk about. We're both adults who find each other attractive. Why can't that be enough for now?" she asked, her heart beginning to race as she waited for his answer.

He finished with Avery's hands and then set Avery down between the two of them so that each could take a hand as the toddler wobbled on her inexperienced legs.

"So, still friends?" he asked as they started back down the path.

"Yes," Hannah answered, letting go of the ball of stress she'd held inside her all day. "Still friends."

As promised, they met Lindsey at the small cat exhibit and William settled Avery in the stroller so that Lindsey could push her to see the big cats.

By the time they'd talked Lindsey into leaving, Avery was tired and cranky.

As they exited the zoo, passing other families headed inside, Hannah couldn't help but note the contrast between those families and her group: a single parent, a fatherless child, an orphaned toddler and her big brother. They were a motley crew, but somehow they fit together perfectly.

William's home had been a nice quiet place when he he'd left it to make morning rounds. His morning had been quite peaceful; he'd worked his way through his patients just the way he liked to.

And then he'd come home to a horror that no man should have to face. His driveway was filled with cars. Cars. On a Sunday. In his driveway. Of course, he'd known that there was to be a birthday party. He and Hannah had picked out the design of the cake at the bakery the week before. Hannah had volunteered to take charge of the invitations and, naïvely, he had thought that meant half a dozen of Hannah's friends would attend with their kids. This was not half a dozen. There were at least a dozen cars here.

Leaving the safety of his silver sedan, he followed the sounds of voices around to the back of the house where pure mayhem seemed to reign. There were children everywhere, some chasing others, some playing on blankets laid out on the grass, and a couple older ones that surrounded Lindsey, one of which was a boy. Had Hannah known that Lindsey was inviting a boy? What were the guidelines for that? Was it one of those things determined by age? Thank goodness, he had a long time till he had to worry about that with Avery.

"Hey, Dr. Cooper. Nice house and a very cute kid," said a nurse he recognized as Kelly from the neuro unit.

"Have you seen, Hannah?" he asked.

"She just went into the house. She'll be right out." He turned to see a dark-haired beauty with a small round belly. She was holding toddler on one hip.

"Sarah. It's nice to see you," he said as he looked around. "Is David with you?"

"He's over there," Sarah said, pointing to a small group of men gathered at the bank of the lake. "I think they're plotting an escape. You can tell my husband that I've got my eye on him. Any attempt to flee before the cake comes out will be a breach of contract."

"Flee?" he asked. If there was any type of escape, he was going to be part of it.

"I accompany him to all those fussy functions you doctors are required to attend and he shows up at all the children functions with me— Davey, you get out of that tree right this minute!" she said before heading off toward a group of children.

William looked to the house and saw that Hannah had come back out. She carried Avery much as Sarah had held her little one, one hip cocked to the side as she balanced a large platter of food in her other hand. But the two women couldn't have been any more different in looks with Sarah's dark waves and Hannah's blond curls.

As he walked toward her, his eyes followed the line of Hannah's curves until they rested on her flat stomach. He knew the story of how Sarah had lost both her husband and her son in a motor vehicle accident. The loss had been devastating and he couldn't imagine that it had been an easy decision for her to have more children. Would Hannah ever want more children? She'd been through so much with Lindsey. Would she be willing to take a chance at having another child?

He watched as Hannah handed the large platter to an older woman. Mrs. Adams?

"I thought we were doing something small for her first birthday," he said as an aside to Hannah after thanking Avery's former nanny for coming.

"You were the one who wanted the blow-up bouncy house. Who did you think was going to bounce in it if we didn't invite some other children? All Avery can do is crawl in there," Hannah said.

"She's the birthday girl. Of course she can bounce in it," William said as he reached for Avery. "Come on, Avery. Let's go try out that house."

"Don't get her dress dirty. We need to get her picture taken with the cake," Hannah called after him.

After waiting their turn, William climbed up into the air-filled house and held the toddler's hands. "Okay, you jump up and down," he said, raising her by her arms then letting her feet touch the bottom.

Avery seemed interested in everything but the bouncy house he'd insisted on renting.

"You know she's too little for that, don't cha, Dr. Cooper. Her legs aren't ready," a young boy said as he stuck his head into the opening. "You should have gotten a pony. Everybody likes to ride a pony, no matter how little they are."

"I think you may be right, Davey." William smiled at Sarah's son as he crawled out of the house with Avery. "Next time I'll get a pony."

He quickly made the basic introductions of Avery to the people he knew from work, then joined the group of men by the lake. They were talking baseball and politics, subjects he found a lot safer than the ones he'd heard the women discussing earlier. Avery held on to his neck as they watched Hannah and Sarah lead groups of children through games he knew Avery wasn't old enough to play.

"So there you are," Hannah said as she approached the group and reached out for Avery. "It's time to cut the cake and we can't do it without her."

William claimed the responsibility for taking pictures of Avery as everyone sang the birthday song and he had to admit that his sister was adorable as she stuffed a piece of rainbow-colored cake into her mouth with both hands. Before he knew what was happening, however, he was organizing various groups for pictures.

"Where's Lindsey?" he asked after snapping a picture of Hannah bent over Avery as she tried to blow out her birthday candles. It would be the perfect picture to use as the new wallpaper on his phone.

"She's with her friends inside. I think," Hannah added as they started to cut the large cake into smaller pieces to hand out to each child.

"There's a boy here," he said to Hannah.

"There're lots of boys here. Avery's too young to want an all-girls party," Hannah laughed.

"No, I mean there's a boy here that's Lindsey's age," William said. "And what's an all-girls party? What am I supposed to do with that?"

"Yes, I know there's a boy here with Lindsey's friends, and you don't need to worry about any all-girls parties for a few years yet."

Both Hannah and William helped Avery open her presents and then, finally, it was all done. As quickly as the presents had been opened, the wrappings were collected, along with the empty cups and leftover food. Everyone pitched in to clean the picnic tables, which apparently had been brought in by various guests. By the time he'd helped load the last table into the back of a truck and thanked Mrs. Adams's son for bringing her, his peaceful yard had been returned to normal.

He picked up a stray can that had been thrown into the fire pit and took a seat in the chair he'd dragged to the edge of the lake the night he had moved into the house. He'd known that the house was too big when he'd bought it, but somehow it had called to him. Something had told him that he belonged there and he had trusted his instincts enough to buy it. He'd immediately taken up fly fishing and though he enjoyed the sport, he'd still felt like something was missing.

Looking out over the lake, William tried to remember a time when he had enjoyed himself that much in his own backyard. Yes, he and the other men had groaned each time one of the women had come to ask for their help. But he'd also seen how the other fathers had kept an eye on their children when, on the surface, it had looked like they were ignoring everything that was going on. He'd kept his own eye on the boy who had followed Lindsey around the yard.

He stood, walked down to the pier and

gazed into the water. His life was changing and he didn't feel as if he had any control over it. But he was becoming more confident in his role as Avery's guardian now. He still had a lot to learn and he knew he'd make mistakes along the way, but the panic he had felt those first few days when he'd been alone with Avery was long gone.

"Hey," Hannah said as she joined him on the pier. "Enjoying the quiet now that everyone's gone?"

"Yeah, that was some party," he said. "Can you tell me again why a child too young to retain any memories of their first birthday needs a party?"

"It wasn't that bad. She might not remember the party, but she'll have the pictures to show her how many people care for her. She definitely had a great time, too. I barely got her bathed and dressed before she fell asleep."

"Thanks for doing that," he said. "I guess I've been out here longer than I thought. And thanks for your help with the party. Those pictures will be just as important to me later on as they will be to her."

He thought of the picture he had on his phone. Would Avery ever see it? Would she even know who Hannah was by the time she looked back at those pictures?

"It's sad, isn't it? That she had to spend her first birthday without her parents. It should have been her mother putting her to bed tonight," Hannah said. She shivered as a cool spring breeze blew across the lake.

William pulled her in front of him and wrapped his arms around her as she settled back against his chest to share the warmth of his body as they looked out over the lake. Catching a glimpse of their reflection in the water, he was taken aback. There was something different about him when Hannah was beside him. It was the way his body relaxed into hers. She had some magic way of bringing the peace to his life that he had always sought. But would it last? Or, like his father, would he soon be bored and looking for someone else to entertain him? He told himself that he wasn't like his father, but inside he feared he might be. He'd spent his life in superficial relationships with women.

"I keep wondering why Avery's mother and my father wanted me to be the one to take care of her if something happened to them. I guess I'll never know," he said as he took Hannah's hand and led her back to the house.

"Maybe the thought of the two of you alone wasn't something they wanted. Maybe they knew that they could count on you to take care of your sister," Hannah said.

"I don't know. It doesn't really matter. I can't change the past."

"But maybe just accepting the possibility that your father might not have been as heartless as you thought he was will be enough for you to let go of the pain you felt as a child. None of us can really know what another person thinks or feels. Maybe just putting to rest those old feelings you still have will help," Hannah suggested, squeezing his hand. "Because it's never too late to forgive someone, is it?"

For the first time in a long time, William felt a spark of hope. He'd never thought he'd be able to forgive his father for divorcing his mother and bringing another woman in to raise him, but maybe it was time to let all of those old feelings go. It was time he moved on with his life and, if it meant forgiving his father, then he was ready to do it. He couldn't hold on to the anger he had felt for so many years while he raised his father's daughter. It wouldn't be fair to let Avery bear the brunt of his negative emotions for a man she would never know. He could unintentionally warp her feelings for her father and that wasn't something William could do to her. If he wanted to raise Avery, he needed to forgive their father.

CHAPTER TWELVE

HANNAH ENTERED THE house to find Lindsey standing with her backpack over her shoulder and her best friend at her side. Suspicious grins on each of their faces set Hannah's mother radar on high alert.

"Jessica's mom is coming to pick us up. She says it's okay if I spend the night there. And I can ride the bus to school with Jessica in the morning. Can I? Please?" Lindsey asked.

"Did you pack all your medications?" Hannah asked.

"Of course, Mom." Lindsey pulled out a bag of medication and shook it as if to show her mother that the bottles weren't empty.

Her daughter had sarcasm down to an art form.

"Is that boy going to be there?" William asked as he followed her inside.

"What boy? You mean Jason?" Lindsey exchanged looks with Jessica before rolling her eyes. "No. And he's just a friend. Of course, sometimes friends become...you know, other things."

"What other things?" William queried.

A horn honked outside and both girls sped out the door. Hannah knew they were up to something. Fortunately, she also knew Jessica's mother well enough to feel confident they would be closely monitored for the night.

"She's too young to know about 'other things,'" William muttered from behind her, making her smile.

It wasn't until Hannah looked across the room that she realized what her adorable, scheming daughter and her friend had been doing while they'd been outside.

A small table had been moved into the center of the room, a vase with flowers she recognized from William's front garden holding center stage. The table had been set for two and there was a note propped against the vase.

"What's this?" William asked as they stood staring at the misplaced furniture.

"I think my daughter is trying to move us on to 'other things,'" Hannah said, laughing when she caught the grin on William's face. "I'm not sure my daughter's idea of 'other things' is the same as yours, though."

"I certainly hope not," he said, picking up the note. "According to this, our supper will be delivered at eight, but it doesn't give any details on what that might be."

"The only thing my daughter can afford on her allowance is pizza, I'm afraid."

Lindsey was such a special child and she was so lucky to be her mom.

Hannah thought of the little girl sleeping down the hall. Already, Avery had showed herself to be a resilient child, settling in comfortably with three strangers. She was silly and happy, but also stubborn. She was so cute in the way that all children her age were with her chubby cheeks and bright eyes, but Hannah could already see that Avery would be a beauty like her mother. William would have his hands full when his sister hit her teens. She'd love to be around to see it, but at this point in her life, Hannah wasn't even sure she'd be in Houston for much longer. But that wasn't something she was going to dwell on tonight.

With Avery down and Lindsey gone, she and William could have this one night to themselves. They had so little time left before she moved back home. She would not let tonight be ruined by things she could do nothing about.

"I'm going to go change. The smell of frosting is starting to get to me," Hannah said as she looked down at her shirt where smears of cake had dried.

"We have a little time before dinner," William said, checking his watch.

She wondered if she should tell him about the clump of frosting on his own shirt. No, let him see it for himself, she thought. Maybe the next time he saw a birthday cake he would think of today and the messy frosting from his little sister's first birthday. And maybe he'd remember her, too.

They parted at the top of the stairs, each headed to their own room.

Hannah quickly went through her closet, sorting through her mommy clothes and work clothes. She wanted William to see her as a woman tonight instead of as a coworker or babysitter. A strong woman that he could count on—something she knew he hadn't had since his mother was taken from him. But she also wanted him to see her as desirable. She wanted William to think of tonight as a date. A first date—the date that always determined whether there would be another.

Reaching to the back corner of the closet, she felt the soft cotton of her favorite floral sundress whose color almost matched the blue of her eyes. It was a little worn, but it would be perfect for tonight.

Glancing at her bedside clock, she rushed to the bathroom. She had just enough time to shower and apply makeup.

When she returned to the main floor, she noticed that the lights had been dimmed. Yet through the soft glow of candles strategically placed in the great room, she could see William sitting in a chair that had been turned to face her. Had he been sitting there just waiting for her? Her heart stuttered when he stood. Dressed in dark slacks and a buttoned chambray shirt, his hair still damp and brushed back from his face, he appeared even more dangerous than normal.

She stepped toward him until they both

stopped just inches from touching. A delicious tingle flowed through Hannah's body as his eyes skimmed over her then settled on her lips. The air between them seemed to spark with a magnetic force that held the two of them in place. Her breasts felt heavy and the muscles at her core contracted, making her breath catch. She wanted to kiss him but they both seemed to know that that would be a mistake. One kiss would never be enough. They had the whole night together. There was no reason to rush things. Not tonight.

The doorbell rang, startling them out of the sensuous trance.

"I'll get it." William stepped away and went to the front door.

Hannah poured herself a glass of wine from the bottle he had opened and took a big sip. Her body trembled with a need she had never felt for any other man. How long had they been standing there? It was as if they could be intimate without even touching. Just the warmth of his gaze was enough to set her body on fire.

"I feel bad that Lindsey paid for our dinner," William said as he set the cardboard box on the table set for just the two of them.

"Why? You've been so great helping her with her homework while I've been busy with my own studies. By the way, she made an A on that history paper you helped her with," Hannah said as she took her seat, opened the box and breathed in the smell of crusty bread and tomato sauce rich with herbs. The only thing she could remember eating today was a piece of Avery's overly sweet birthday cake. She took two pieces of the pizza without even considering the calories. Hopefully, she'd burn it off later tonight.

"She's a smart kid," he said, taking his seat.

"She's had a lot of catching up to do after so much time in hospital. Lindsey missed so much school while she was sick that she's had to have tutoring for the last two summers. But she's finally catching up with her classmates," Hannah said.

As they ate, she told him about the particular heart defect Lindsey had been born with and the number of surgeries and complications she'd overcome. When they'd finished their meal, neither one seemed ready to rush the time they had together.

"You've done a great job with her," William said. "Your parents have to see that."

How could she explain her parents to him when she didn't even understand them herself?

"When Lindsey was born with a heart defect, my parents felt that it would be best if I let someone older, with more support, raise her," she said. *Not that they'd ever offered to help.* Then again, that had never been the plan.

Hannah's stomach twisted as she was reminded of the secret she'd hidden away. William wouldn't consider her such a wonderful mother if he knew—

But keeping the truth from him didn't seem right. She wanted him to know the real her, warts and all. Would he look at her differently when he learned the truth? There was only one way to find out.

"Lindsey doesn't know this…but the plan was never for me to keep her," Hannah told him. This was this one terrible truth that had haunted her as her child had lain sick and at times close to death. Who would have been there beside her child if she had let her parents have their way?

Hannah took a large swallow of wine before continuing. "When I came home from college and told my parents that I was pregnant and the father did not want to be involved, they arranged for a couple in their church to adopt the baby. A private adoption…

"I shouldn't have been surprised. They'd always controlled my life and I'd never been given the freedom that my friends had. My parents didn't see it as any different from deciding what college I would attend."

She paused as if to take a calming breath. "When I found out about the adoption arrangements, I was angry. I pushed back as hard as I could, but eventually they convinced me that the best thing for my child was for me to give her parents who could provide for her.

"I'm not trying to put all the blame on them," she quickly added. "I had the final decision on what I would do. I knew I had nothing to offer a child. I was the one who had been willing to give my daughter up. I was the one who would have signed the papers to give my daughter away."

"You were young, Hannah. Your parents made some good points," William said.

"I know, and sometimes I can convince myself of that. But when Lindsey was born with a heart defect and the family that was supposed to adopt her backed out, I knew I couldn't give my baby up.

"My parents refused to understand why I insisted on keeping her. That's when I realized that what they really wanted was for us all to pretend that Lindsey had never happened. They wanted me to leave her at the hospital, where she would have gone into foster care if another couple couldn't have been found by the adoption agency. I refused, and they wouldn't support my decision. Hannah took a sip from her wineglass. "It's only been in the last year that they've showed any sign of wanting to be a part of our lives."

It still hurt to admit that her parents had abandoned not only their granddaughter, but also their own child. It had taken years for Hannah to come to terms with the fact that her parents had controlled her whole life up until the moment she had walked out with Lindsey. Part of her had thought they would come after her, that they would change their minds, but they were too proud for that. They would never admit that they had made a mistake.

The two of them sat in silence for a moment. Some of the candles had burned down, leaving the room in almost total darkness.

She had told him everything now.

"I've never regretted the decision I made to keep my daughter, William, even though there were times I wasn't sure how we were going to make it. I wouldn't have been able to live with myself if I had walked away and left her in that hospital. Just like I know you wouldn't have been able to live with yourself if you had turned your back on Avery."

"Hannah, you are one special lady," William said.

"And you are one special man."

"I'm not—" he said, stopping when she put a finger to his lips.

"To me, you are. And that's all that matters tonight."

William nipped at her finger and she drew it back and placed it in her mouth. His eyes blazed with heat as candlelight flickered across them. He held his hand out for hers and she gave it to him, mesmerized as he raised it to his lips and kissed each fingertip.

This was the man no one else knew. Right now, he was *her* William. Tomorrow he'd step back into the shoes of the William others knew as the ice-cold neurosurgeon. But that was tomorrow. Tonight, he was all hers.

They stood and she stepped into his arms as he reached for her. The first time they had made love, they had both been desperate. This time, she wanted to take her time as she loved him with her body. She would give him the tenderness of her lips, the warmth of her breasts, and the sweet completeness of their joining. They'd made no promises to each other. Tonight would be special, and they both knew it. She would make sure that he would never forget this night.

Hannah kissed him lightly on the lips before pulling away and taking his hand.

"My room," she said as they got to the top of the stairs. For some reason, the choice mattered to her. Home advantage? Maybe, she thought as she shut the door behind them so they wouldn't disturb Avery.

As the door clicked softly into place, strong arms surrounded her. She turned into them as William pulled her close. His lips met hers as he held her tightly against him. She could feel every inch of his hard body. Wrapping her arms around his neck, Hannah ran her hands into his hair and gave over her mouth to him. His tongue tangled with hers and her body shuddered. She'd thought she could control this need they had for each other. She'd been wrong.

"Too many clothes," he said, his lips leaving hers and his hands reaching behind her for the zipper of her dress.

"Yes," she said as she pulled back and began to work the buttons of his shirt.

Hannah felt the cool air against her skin as her dress landed at her feet. She pulled the shirt loose from his pants and ran her hands up the strong chest she had not been able to forget since that first night in the gym.

William's clothes quickly followed hers to the floor as they touched and tasted, each taking the time to explore. He moaned when she grazed his nipple with her teeth. He returned the torment as he cupped her breasts and tortured each nipple with his tongue.

He lifted her into his arms and lay her on

the bed before returning to his pants to retrieve something from his wallet.

When he was back beside her, Hannah opened herself to him and welcomed him into her. She sighed with contentment as he covered her body with his. Never had she felt so complete, so whole. Reaching up, she pulled his head down and looked into eyes that spoke of something she knew he wasn't prepared to confess.

Did he see that same desperate emotion in her eyes? What if she said the words she knew he didn't want to hear? Would it push him away? Did he know he filled not only her body but also her heart? She had to take the chance. She had to tell him.

"William, I—" His lips crushed hers, taking the words she would give him away.

All thought left her. He moved inside her, but not with the slow, gentle loving he'd showed her before. Gone was that gentle lover, replaced by a man who demanded that she give him total possession of her body. He drove himself into her with a desperate need she answered with her own.

Arching into him, Hannah wrapped her legs around his hips, pulling him closer as her body began to tremble. Holding back nothing, she screamed as the force of the climax took over. Still, William thrust inside her, claiming her body as he took everything she had to give until he joined her in completion.

CHAPTER THIRTEEN

SOMEONE HAD HOLD of his face. Groaning, William turned his head away only to have two small hands turn it back. So that was how the game was played. He turned his head the other way and Avery giggled then turned it back toward her. He wiggled his mouth back and forth and the giggling increased as the toddler patted his cheeks. Opening his eyes, he was greeted with deep brown ones that were all but plastered to his face.

"Good morning, Avery. And how did you manage to get in here?" he asked. He'd been so busy trying to catch up in his role as Avery's substitute parent that he hadn't thought about what having a young child in the house would mean for his sex life. He couldn't imagine any of the women he had dated being happy about his new role. If there was one thing he'd learned from his father's experiences, it was that women did not like to share a man's attention with anyone else.

"She woke up in the night and I just let her sleep with us," Hannah called out from the open bathroom door.

"Probably too much partying last night," William joked as he moved Avery over to the other side of the bed while he sat up and re-arranged the comforter. "I'm sorry I didn't hear her."

He didn't make it a practice to wake up in a women's bed and the few times he had, it had been extremely awkward for both him and the woman. Somehow, this morning didn't feel that way. It was just another day for the two of them to juggle childcare and work. And that was Hannah's doing. She always seemed to know what he needed from her.

He'd sworn he'd keep her out of his life, but somehow she'd found a way inside the walls he'd constructed to keep others out. She now knew more about him than any other person. Having someone know all your secrets was somehow liberating. And that definitely sur-prised him. He'd always been afraid to share that much of himself with anyone.

"Too much sugar," Hannah said before he heard the hair dryer turn on.

William remembered the first three nights Avery had been with him. They had both been miserable, neither getting much sleep. The giggling child who was now playing with a stuffed toy was much more appealing than the one who'd cried continuously every time he had tried to get her to go to sleep in the small cot her nanny had dropped off with her. He'd ordered a crib as soon as the store had opened the next day. It hadn't helped.

It had only been when Hannah had moved in that the situation had improved. She'd had the answer to every problem…and now she had shared hers with him. He wasn't the same man he had been then. With Hannah's help, he'd learned to take care of Avery as well as any other father could.

"It was her birthday. Of course she had too much sugar," he said as Hannah stepped into the room. She'd already dressed in scrubs for her day in the office yet she looked just as beautiful as she had last night when they'd dressed up for dinner. He found her beauty a soft gentle thing that tugged at his heart as well as his body—

His mind came to a screeching halt. Was he somehow romanticizing this thing between them? Just because he was more comfortable around her than he'd ever been around another person didn't mean there was a future for them. That wasn't the plan.

The plan had never included becoming lovers, either.

"She hasn't woken in the middle of the night in weeks, so I wouldn't worry about it." Hannah reached down and picked Avery up. "I'll feed her this morning while you get ready. I would have woken you earlier, but I knew your first appointment this morning wasn't till nine, so you should have time to do your rounds before you come to the office."

He looked over at the clock on the bedside table as Hannah left the room. He had no idea where this thing between them was going. He'd been honest with her concerning the future he had seen for himself before Avery had come into his life. Now the thought of the empty life he'd planned seemed to be losing some of its appeal.

Last night they had found a passion he had never experienced before. One that had driven Hannah to almost whisper those three words that had always sent him running. Words she would have regretted once her body had been satisfied and her mind had cleared. Words she wouldn't have been able to take back once she'd said them. Words that hurt when they weren't returned.

He'd refused to hear them, choosing instead to protect her from the pain she would have felt this morning. If one person could understand why he didn't believe in the love all the romantics talked about, it was Hannah. She knew he had no belief in the happily-ever-after love his father had promised not one, but four different brides. William might be able to forgive his father for moving on with his life after his mother's accident, but that didn't mean he could change what he had seen and experienced in the name of love.

William picked his pants up from the floor where he had dropped them and headed for the shower. Maybe the best thing was for them both to ignore what was happening between them. If he was lucky, his day would be a busy one with no time to think about the night before, because there was a part of him that couldn't help but wonder what might have happened if he'd been brave enough to let Hannah say those three little words. And that was a thought that scared him to death.

"Hannah!" Mrs. Nabors called out as Marion walked her and her daughter along the hall to an examination room.

"Mrs. Nabors, how are you doing?" Hannah inquired, giving the woman a hug. "You look great."

"The rehab has really helped," Lisa, her daughter, said.

"I can take them," Hannah told Marion. While still not singing her praises, the older nurse had stopped hounding Hannah about everything she did.

"So you're not working at the hospital anymore?" Lisa asked as Hannah settled them into the room.

"I've taken some time off to complete my remaining clinical hours for my bachelor's degree. That's why I'm working here with Dr. Cooper," Hannah said as she applied the blood pressure cuff to Mrs. Nabors's arm.

"Well, you're working for one of the best," the older woman said. "And he's such a nice young man—"

A door slammed down the hall and she heard Marion cry out. Had she fallen?

"I'll be right back," Hannah said before rushing out of the room.

Expecting to see the nurse on the floor, she dashed around the corner of the hall and stopped. Marion was leaning back against the wall opposite a man Hannah recognized as Jeannine Jones's husband. She glanced at Marion. "Did he hurt you?"

Marion shook her head, though Hannah could see that she was cradling her arm.

"What is it you want, Mr. Jones?" Hannah asked. His wife had been moved out of the critical care department only the day before with strict orders that he was not to visit once they had learned he'd been released on bond. Surely, the staff had not let him in to see her.

"I want to see the doctor that's told those nurses I couldn't see my wife. And I want to see him now!"

William had been on a call for a consult with another doctor earlier, but she knew he'd be out at any minute. In the mood that Calvin Jones was in, there was no telling what he would do. She needed to notify the security officers that minded the entrance of the office complex without letting him know what she was doing.

"Dr. Cooper is over at the hospital making rounds. I'll call him and let him know you want to talk to him. I'm sure there's been some mistake," Hannah said as she took her phone out of her pocket and dialed the building's security number.

The phone was answered on the second ring. "Hey Dr. Cooper, Jeannine Jones's husband is here in the office and wants to talk to you." She listened as a man told her she had the wrong number. "I understand you're busy, Dr. Cooper, but Mr. Jones is very upset about his wife refusing to go home with him. Thank you, I'll let him know you'll be right here."

She hit the end call button and prayed that the security officer she'd talked to had understood that she needed help.

"The doctor will be here in just a few minutes. I'll show you to a room where you can wait for him," Hannah said. She needed to get Mr. Jones out of the hall and away from Marion.

"I'm not going anywhere till I see that doctor. He had no business talking to my wife when I wasn't there. Thinks just because he's got some degree that he knows what's best for everyone. I'll make sure he keeps his nose out of our business from now on," Jones said. "And you! You're that nurse who wouldn't let me into the room to see my wife that day in the ER. You called those guards on me. You're just as bad as he is."

Calvin Jones pushed past Marion and headed for Hannah. He thought he could intimidate her just as he had his poor wife. She wouldn't give him the satisfaction. She was tired of dealing with this bully. He'd beaten his wife until she was scared to tell the truth about the horror of her marriage. He preyed on the weak, but that wasn't who Hannah was anymore. She would stand up to this man just as she had stood up to her parents the day she had refused to leave the hospital without her daughter.

"Mr. Jones, I was only doing my job. Just like Dr. Cooper is doing his job to protect his patient. It would be best if you left right now before you do something that's going to cause more trouble for you. It's my understanding that there is a restraining order that states you aren't allowed to see your wife," Hannah said calmly as the man approached her.

She yelled as he grabbed hold of her hair and pulled her up to her toes. "Lady, if you know what's good for you, you'll stay away from my wife. And I'm not going anywhere until I see the doctor."

"Let her go. Now!" Hannah heard William give the order from behind her. "If you have a problem with me, we can discuss it like men."

Hannah's head slammed into the wall as Calvin Jones pushed her away and stalked toward William. Marion reached her before she hit the floor then held her back as she fought to go after him.

She saw the ice-cold determination in William's eyes. "I'm going to give you one opportunity to walk out of the office," he said calmly, as if talking to someone about the weather. "I'm not a violent man, but I'm twenty years younger than you and I'm willing to take my chances."

The man snarled a comment that Hannah couldn't hear before two officers pushed through into the office. Hannah tried to yell out as she saw Jeannine's husband lunge at William. And then it all disappeared into black.

* * *

Hannah opened her eyes slowly and realized someone was holding her down. Staring up at the white-tiled ceiling of an exam room, she tried to recall how she had gotten there. The pounding of her head brought back the memory of hitting something. The wall. She'd hit the wall before Jeannine's husband had attacked William. "William," she said as she tried to sit up before falling back to the table as the room began to spin.

"It's okay. I'm right here," William said from beside her.

Turning her head slowly, Hannah reached out for him. "You're okay," she said as he took her hand. She put her other hand on his face and turned it side to side. There was no damage.

"I thought I saw him hit you," she said, closing her eyes again. The lights were too bright.

"I'm fine. The man is all brute and no style," he said. "How are you feeling?"

"My head is killing me, but besides that, I think I'm okay." Her roiling stomach felt as if she had just gotten off a carnival ride, but she knew it was because of the pain in her head.

"The cops are talking to Marion and there's an ambulance on its way to take you to the ER," William said.

"I just need something for this headache," she said, turning toward him. The room spun once more.

"You know as well as I do that you need to get checked out. They'll get a CT just to make sure you're okay." The door opened and two emergency medical technicians came in with a stretcher. "Now, be nice and don't give these young men any trouble," William told.

William stood beside the CT technician and watched as the screens changed from one view to the next. He'd confirm his findings with the radiologist, but it appeared that Hannah had not received any type of brain or cranial injury.

When he'd seen Jeannine's husband throw her against that wall, he had experienced an anger that he had never known before. Part of him even wished he'd had a chance to punch the man. He'd given his statement to the police officers who had arrived with the ambulance crew and had promised to call them when Hannah was up to talking, but it wasn't enough.

William wanted to know that Calvin Jones was going to spend some time in a cell for what he'd done to Hannah today. He wanted to know the man wouldn't be able to come after Hannah—or his wife—again. Unfortunately, the officers hadn't been able to reassure him.

Marion had given her report to the police before she'd been sent off to get her arm x-rayed. From what his office nurse had said, it seemed that Hannah had been trying to keep Calvin Jones from knowing that he was in the office. She'd tried to protect him; something he couldn't remember anyone else ever doing in his life. She'd taken on a man as strong as an ox for him. He would never forget that and he'd never forget the fear he'd felt when she'd lost consciousness.

William's mind had immediately imagined the worst, fearing that Hannah had sustained the same type of injury his mother had. What would he have done had she been critically injured? He'd been the neuro trauma doctor on call, but he would never have trusted himself to operate on her. Because no matter how much he could compartmentalize his emotions while he was in the operating room, there was no way he could have done that if Hannah had been his patient.

He took one more look at the CT before leaving the room. Thank goodness, it wasn't anything he had to worry about now. He was going to find the ER doctor and get the paperwork started to take Hannah home.

CHAPTER FOURTEEN

"Sit down, Momma," Lindsey said for the hundredth time as Hannah stood then quickly sank back down on the couch. It had been two days since she'd been attacked and still her daughter and William wouldn't let her do anything.

William had canceled his office visits today and had arranged for a colleague to make the rounds on his surgical patients. He didn't know it yet, but Hannah was going to assist him in the scheduled surgeries tomorrow. The ER doctor had cleared her to return to work and she wasn't about to miss a chance to be inside the OR.

With her headache now gone, there really wasn't any reason she couldn't get back to normal. Not that she was protesting their protectiveness. It felt nice to know that she had someone to take care of her for a change. With her down for the count, William had been glad to take over care of Lindsey. He'd even taken care of her carpool duties for the day.

"Will, what temperature does it say that the oven needs to be on?" Lindsey asked, pulling out a large round pan.

"Four fifty," he said as Avery's hands stretched out to touch the dough he had been meticulously rolling.

Reaching into a bowl, he picked out a slice of a sweet bell pepper and gave it to her to chew on. After one taste, Avery threw it to the floor. "Apparently she's not a fan of peppers."

"Try the pepperoni," Hannah said as she took in the mess the kitchen was becoming. For a man who was meticulous in the operating room, he was a disaster in the kitchen.

William put Avery in the high chair and handed her a slice of pepperoni. "Sit here for just a minute while I get the pizza in the oven."

"Ill, Ill," the little girl called when he crossed to the other side of the island.

"Ill?" he asked as he carefully took the

dough from a wooden board and placed it on a round baking tray. "That's a new one."

"She's trying to say 'Will,' you dork," Lindsey said.

"Lindsey, don't call William a dork. It's not polite." Hannah had a hard time keeping the smile off her face.

"Forget about it, Lindsey. I can't have my sister going around calling me 'Ill.' What kind of name is that for a doctor?" William joked.

"It's better than Billy," Lindsey quipped as they began layering the meat and veggies they'd managed to agree on.

"Not by much," William said. "We'll have to work on that vocabulary of yours, little sister."

"Ill," Avery said, reaching for him again.

"Let me get the pie in the oven, then you can get down," he said to Avery then turned to Hannah. "Isn't it time for her to start walking? She's been pulling up on things for a while now. Maybe I should check with the pediatrician…"

The doorbell rang and Lindsey bolted for it. "I'll get it," she called back to them.

"It's a little late for a delivery driver," William said, putting the pizza in the oven and setting the timer. "Maybe I should go see who it is."

"I'll go," Hannah said as she started to stand. She was starting to feel a little guilty. She really did feel better.

She looked over at the kitchen counter covered in flour. *Perhaps one more day of rest won't hurt.*

An odd feeling settled in his stomach. "Stay with Avery. I'll be right back," William said to Hannah.

There was no good reason for someone to be at the door at this time of night. There was only one person he had been expecting at his home. The text he had received from his father's lawyer earlier in the week had been sent to prepare him, but he had chosen to ignore it. With Hannah injured, he hadn't wanted to deal with anything that would upset her. And, he had to admit—even if it was just to himself—this was likely going to upset them all.

"Will, this woman says she's here to see Avery," Lindsey said when he entered the hallway, her arms crossed at her chest. He had seen that look on her mother's face often enough to know it always meant trouble. "Is she that aunt I heard you and Momma talking about—the one who thinks you can't take care of Avery?"

"Ms. Crane?" he asked the woman standing in the open doorway. His heart rate sped up as the woman nodded. Why was she here?

"Lindsey," Will said as he placed his arm around her shoulders, "this is Avery's great-aunt."

"I'm sorry it's so late, but I only just managed to make it to town and I couldn't wait to see Alison's little girl," the woman said as Lindsey slipped from under his arm and bolted to the great room.

She was dressed in tasteful but sensible clothes, reminding William of Avery's former nanny, Mrs. Adams. Though much older than his stepmother, he could see the resemblance.

"Please come in." William stepped back, welcoming her into his home.

He looked to the high chair where Avery had been just minutes before and found it empty.

"This is Hannah, Lindsey's mother." He introduced her as she joined them. "Hannah, this is Avery's great-aunt—" The oven timer went off. "Let me get that."

Hannah led the woman into the great room. "Please, have a seat," she said, surprising him with the control she seemed to have of her emotions. If the woman's arrival had upset her, Hannah sure wasn't showing it. "You must be tired. William says you raised Avery's mother. This must be so hard for you."

"Yes. I'm still in a bit of a shock, I'm afraid. Alison was so young. I didn't find out till the ship I was on made port, and by then I had missed the funeral. Of course, I wish I had been there for Avery. It's like history repeating itself. Though, Alison was much older when we lost her parents."

Ms. Crane looked around the room where toys covered the rug and a basket of clean clothes sat in a corner waiting to be folded and put away. By the look in her eyes, she was not impressed. What did the woman expect when she showed up unannounced?

William pushed a bowl to the side and set the hot pizza pan on the counter. Yes, the kitchen was a mess, too, but he wasn't going to apologize for it. "We're having homemade pizza for dinner if you would like to join us."

"That sounds nice, but I'm afraid I can't. Spicy food before bed just doesn't agree with me." She stood. "And as you said, it is getting late. I just wanted to spend a minute or two with the child."

"When was the last time you saw Avery?" Hannah asked, walking around to the side of the kitchen where he stood. She poked him in the side. He ignored her. He knew Alison's aunt was there to check him out, to judge how well he was caring for Avery. It wasn't like he could throw her out. He needed to show her that Avery was well and happy.

"The last time I visited Dallas was right after she was born. She was such a cute little thing. Alison was so proud of her," Ms. Crane said.

"She's a beautiful little girl and she's just crazy about her big brother," Hannah said.

"I'm sure she is, dear, but I'm also sure you can understand my concern for my Alison's only child. My niece would expect me to make sure that her daughter was being taken care of properly," she said. "There's only the two of us left in the family now that Alison is gone."

William looked at the woman and realized

that, like him, she was all alone, except for Avery. He didn't have to imagine how lonely she might feel. He knew. He'd felt that way himself, though he'd convinced himself that he liked his life that way.

"Avery has already been put down for the night, but we'd love to have you over for dinner tomorrow night, if that would work for you?" Hannah said, turning on her Texas charm. She was up to something, but William wasn't sure exactly what.

The woman hesitated for a moment then nodded. "Tomorrow night would be lovely. It will give us a chance to talk about our plans for Avery."

After agreeing on a time for dinner the next night, William showed her out then waited until the car turned out of the driveway.

When he returned to the kitchen, he found Hannah surveying the room.

"You need to rest," he said, though he knew he was wasting his breath.

"We don't have time to rest. It would have been best if I'd invited her the night after, but I don't think we could have put her off that long," Hannah said as she started loading the dishwasher.

"She seems like a nice woman," he said.

"A nice woman that wants to talk about plans to take your sister away," Hannah retorted.

"You make it sound like we're going to war."

"What is more important than fighting for your child?" Hannah asked. "Go upstairs and get Lindsey and Avery. We have a dinner to prepare for. By the time she leaves tomorrow night, you'll have Avery's great-aunt singing your praises and putting your name in for father of the year."

"How about we just settle on convincing her that Avery is being properly taken care of?" William suggested as he left the room. Because if Avery's great-aunt really cared about her, it wouldn't matter if the floor was cluttered with toys or what the state of his kitchen was. The only thing that would really matter was that Avery was healthy and happy. Hopefully, the woman was smart enough to understand that.

"Lindsey, please open the door," William said as he knocked for the second time.

"Is that woman gone?" she asked, unlocking the door to let him in.

Avery was sitting on the floor playing with a stuffed unicorn he recognized as one of Lindsey's. Chewing on the stuffed animal's horn, his sister giggled up at him.

"She's not really going to try to take Avery away, is she?" Lindsey asked as she joined Avery on the floor.

He sat next to her and crossed his long legs. "No one is going to take Avery anywhere," he said and prayed that it was true. His lawyer had assured him that he had a strong case for keeping custody of his sister, unless Avery's great-aunt could show that the child was in danger or neglected, which certainly wasn't the case.

"Look, your momma has invited Ms. Crane over for supper tomorrow night. She'll come and see how great Avery is doing and then she'll leave," William said. "But in the meantime, we need to go help your mother get things together for tomorrow night. Okay?"

"Okay. Let's go, Avery," Lindsey said to the little girl as William rose with her in his arms. "We'll show that great-aunt of yours just how great a dad William is, even though it's kind of weird that he's your brother, too."

William looked down at the young girl and laughed. Like daughter, like mother. The two of them had fought together since the day Lindsey was born. First to stay together and then just for Lindsey to stay alive. He couldn't think of any two people he'd rather have on his side.

CHAPTER FIFTEEN

THE TABLE WAS SET. The kids were bathed and dressed appropriately. There was not one piece of laundry in sight. The battlefield was ready for whatever Ms. Crane threw at them and still Hannah felt she wasn't ready. This was so important. They couldn't mess this up.

She looked over to where Avery stood holding on to the couch as she slowly made her way across to the lone toy on the far cushion. William had protested when Hannah had moved all the toys out of the room. He'd felt that Avery's aunt needed to see the real environment that they had made for Avery. But she had seen the way the woman had looked at the disarray of the great room the night before.

"How old was Alison when she went to live with her aunt?" Hannah asked him, once again straightening one of the placemats. Should she have gone with the white linen she had found in the dining room cabinet, or were the dark blue ones they usually used okay? It had seemed a bit much to bring out all the white linen for the cozy family meal they were about to host.

"Nine? Ten? I'm not sure. But I know that Alison lived with her for many years. Why?" William asked as he knotted his tie.

"Did her aunt have any children of her own?" Hannah she straightened another place setting.

"I don't think so. If she did, the lawyers didn't say anything about them when I asked for information on Alison's family. As far as I know, it was only the two of them after the death of Alison's parents. Is that important?" he queried.

"It just seemed to me that she looked awfully shocked at the mess in the room last night. If she'd ever raised a toddler, she'd have known to expect the mess, wouldn't she?" Hannah began checking the silverware for water spots.

"I can tell you that I had no idea that such a small child could create such a mess, let alone how much garbage," William said. "You might not realize it, but I've always been a bit of a neat freak."

She rolled her eyes and he laughed. He might have relaxed his standards on housekeeping in the house now that Avery was there, but he hadn't changed one bit at work.

The doorbell rang.

"It's showtime," Hannah said as they heard Lindsey holler that she would get the door.

William picked Avery up and started toward the door, but Hannah held him back. "Let her do it. She knows how important tonight is for you. She'll behave."

"We are so happy that you could join us tonight," she heard her daughter say in her most adult-sounding voice as she came into the great room, Ms. Crane at her side.

"It was lovely to be invited. You have a very charming daughter, Hannah. You must be very proud of her. Most young people today have no manners," Ms. Crane said.

"Thank you. I am very proud of my daughter," Hannah said. Not that the young girl dressed in a soft pink shirt and black skirt, resembled the daughter she was used to. "And I'm sure you know this little girl."

Ms. Crane reached out to take Avery and Hannah reluctantly released her. She knew they had to make a point of welcoming Avery's great-aunt, but the mere act of handing over the little girl put Hannah's mother instincts on high alert. She tamped down her need to protect Avery.

Dressed in a butter-yellow sundress, her hair combed into soft, dark curls, the child looked like an angel. "Oh, you poor child. I know you must miss your mommy so much," her great-aunt said as tears appeared in her eyes. "I'm sorry," she said to William and Hannah. "It's still so hard for me to accept that Alison is gone. She was so young."

"It's okay," William responded. "We understand."

"Of course. It's a loss for both of us," she said to William. There was nothing as powerful as grief to forge a bond between two people.

Avery studied the woman holding her with dark, curious eyes. Was there something about her that reminded Avery of her mother? Suddenly she held her two chubby hands out. "Ill," she said, reaching for William.

"It's okay, baby girl. This is your momma's aunt," William soothed as he patted Avery's back. "Ms. Crane, if you wouldn't mind, would you put Avery in her high chair? I'm just going to help get the food on the table."

While not as enjoyable or relaxed a meal as he'd come to expect with Lindsey's persistent questions and Avery's boisterous laughter, William felt confident they were making an impression Ms. Crane—or "Maria" as she had asked them to call her. While they'd danced around the subject of Avery's future during the meal, she'd asked questions about William's practice and how the little girl had settled into her childcare.

"And how about you, Hannah? I take it that you've worked with other children, besides your daughter, of course?" The woman gave Lindsey a smile. "I'm sure William checked your references before you were hired."

Realizing the misunderstanding, William answered before Hannah. "I'm sorry, Maria. I think there's a bit of a misunderstanding. Hannah's not a nanny."

"I'm a nurse, Maria. I'm actually finishing my classes for my nurse practitioner's license this month," Hannah said.

"I'm sorry. I didn't realize that the two of you were involved. I just assumed that William would have to have someone living here to help with Avery," Maria said.

"Hannah's a good friend who agreed to help me till I could get comfortable with taking care of Avery and balancing it with my work. She's been a great teacher. I don't know what I would have done without her," William said. He'd never said words that were any truer.

"Well, that was so nice of you, Hannah," Maria said as she turned to her. "And what an exciting time for you. What are your plans, dear?"

"I'm not sure yet. My goal is to work with one of the neurology practices in town," Hannah told her. "I've been so busy with my course that I haven't had time to start putting in any applications, though."

"Well, I do hope things work out for you, and I so appreciate the care you've given Avery. I'm sure William will miss your help," Maria said. "I have to admit that, after last night, I had my doubts. But still, William, it has to have been hard having Avery to look after while still maintaining your practice.

Are you sure that this is what you want? You're a young man. You need to think about starting a family of your own. Won't Avery be a problem? Not every woman wants to take on another woman's child."

The anger he felt every time someone tried to pressure him into a future they insisted he needed rose again. "I think we're talking about two different things, Maria. My care for my baby sister is the most important thing in my life. I can provide everything Avery needs on my own. We don't need anyone else. Yes, my life has changed. So has Avery's. But we're going to make it."

The table went quiet. Even Avery stopped her jabbering for a moment.

He heard a giggle and looked over just in time to see Avery throw one of the carrots on her plate at Lindsey. "Avery, we don't throw our food," he said calmly.

Rising to take his sister out of her high chair, he announced, "I'm going to take her upstairs. If you'll excuse me, I'll get her ready for bed. It's well past her bedtime and she'll be fussy in the morning if she doesn't get enough sleep. I'll bring her down in a few minutes to say good-night."

"May I be excused, too?" Lindsey asked her mother. "I need to get back to my homework."

Hannah nodded then sat back and looked at Maria. "You have to understand," she began, "how hard William has worked to make a place in his life for Avery. When I first came here, he was a mess. But he was determined to do right by Avery. You'll never find a man as dedicated to a child as he is to his sister. I believe that Avery is good for him, and he is definitely good for her. I can't say I understand your loss, but don't let your sorrow over losing Alison get confused with what is best for Avery."

"But I miss Alison so much," the older woman said, her voice quivering with emotion. "I just want to make sure that her daughter is taken care of properly. She's all I have left."

Hannah took Maria's hand in hers. "You don't need to worry. I promise you, there's not another person in this world who wants that more than William. She's safe with him, Maria. She's all he has, too. And he'll always protect her. With his life, if it should come to that."

Hannah quietly stood and began clearing the table, surprised when Maria asked if she could help.

The woman barely spoke while they worked.

"I didn't mean to imply that William wasn't capable of taking care of Avery," she finally said as she helped load the dishwasher. "I realize times have changed and there are a lot of single men that are responsible for their children. It's just that, from what my niece said, I didn't think William would be one of those men."

"What did Alison say that made you think that?" Hannah asked. She felt her temper begin to flair. William's stepmother had barely known him.

"It wasn't that she said anything bad. It's just that I inquired about him when I came down to see Avery and Alison told me she'd hardly even met him. She said that he seemed to prefer his life by himself...

"I thought that when I arrived in town I would find someone glad to give over the responsibility of my great-niece. Instead, I find a man who has embraced his new life," Maria said. "While I admit I'm a bit sad that I won't be taking Avery home with me, I'm

242 THE NEUROSURGEON'S UNEXPECTED FAMILY

glad they're doing well together. I would never want to cause them any trouble."

Hannah felt the knots she'd had in her stomach all night relax. He'd done it! Maria wouldn't be giving William any problems as far as Avery's custody was concerned.

"Well, we're ready for bedtime now. I thought you might want to say good-night to her before you left," William said as he came up behind them. The smile on his face made it clear he had heard Maria's words.

"You are such a precious child," the woman told Avery as she hugged the toddler to her. As if to comfort the woman, Avery patted her back with one chubby little hand.

"It's okay, little one. You're in good hands," Maria said then looked at William. "I would like to come see her whenever I can get here to visit."

"You're always welcome," William assured her as he took Avery back into his arms. "She'll need you to tell her about her mother when she gets older."

Assured of her welcome the next time she was in town, William and Avery showed Maria out while Hannah headed upstairs to check on Lindsey.

Mingled in with the happiness she felt for William and Avery was the knowledge that they wouldn't need her anymore. William was ready to go it on his own now. Hannah just needed to find the strength to leave him. Her job here was done.

William laid a sleeping Avery down then sat on the chair beside her bed and looked around the room. It was hard for him to remember how the place had looked before it had become Avery's nursery. Had it only been a few months since Mrs. Adams had pushed the little girl into his arms then driven away? His life had changed so much since then. First with the arrival of Avery and then with Hannah and Lindsey. His quiet, orderly sanctuary had quickly turned into a loud, disorderly home. And the surprising thing was, he'd loved every minute of it.

He saw that Lindsey's light was still on as he left Avery's room and knocked on her door. "May I come in?"

"Sure," Lindsey said. She was sitting cross-legged on her bed with books and clothes piled around her.

"Having trouble sleeping?" he asked from the doorway.

"Did you mean it when you said you didn't need anyone besides Avery?" the little girl asked.

Was that really what he had said? He'd wanted Maria to know that he could take care of Avery. He hadn't meant to make Lindsey feel as if she didn't matter to him. If anything, having Hannah and Lindsey in the house had made him see that he did need other people. But he could tell by the sadness in her eyes, eyes so like her mother's, that he had hurt her. "I didn't mean that I don't care about you and your mother. I just meant that I could take care of Avery on my own."

"So you don't need me and Momma to help with Avery anymore? That means it's time for us to leave," Lindsey said, her whole attention on him as he crossed the room.

"What's this?" he asked as he picked up a large album from the bed. Opening it, he saw pictures of houses cut from magazines and papers. Flipping through, he could see where the first pictures had been of small cottages that had been gradually advanced to pictures of full-size houses.

"That's our wish book—mine and Momma's. We've had it as long as I can remember. When we see a picture of a house we like, we put it in the album. Momma says that soon we'll be able to have a house of our own, just like one of these," she said as she turned the page to a nice brick house with a fenced-in yard. "Then she says I can have a dog."

William could see how much this meant to both Lindsey and her mother. Hannah had worked hard to make it as a single mother. She had a dream of providing a home for her daughter. A dream from the album that spoke of many nights combing through magazines looking for that special place for the two of them and she had almost reached that point in her career when it would be possible. Lindsey was right. There wasn't any reason for them to stay now. He'd asked Hannah to teach him how to take care of his sister and she had. That had been the agreement. He couldn't hold her here any longer.

CHAPTER SIXTEEN

IT HAD BEEN a week since they had moved out and William didn't know how much more of this quiet house he could take. He'd marked off each day on the calendar Hannah had insisted they hang on the refrigerator. Each day he'd missed them a little bit more until now there was a physical pain in his chest.

He went through the motions at work, his office seeming empty now that Hannah had also completed her time with him. Each afternoon he came home with Avery and did his best to keep his mood as upbeat as possible for his sister. Each night he tossed in his bed and wished that Hannah was beside him.

Where was that peace he had felt when his house had been quiet and orderly? He'd been happy with his life before.

He'd made it clear to Hannah from the beginning that he wasn't one of those men who believed he had to have a woman in his life to complete him. But that had been before he'd realized what a lonely existence his life was without Hannah and Lindsey. He'd been stubborn and had needed to prove to himself that he didn't need someone to help him with Avery. He'd had to prove that he wasn't like his father, that he didn't always need a woman just to exist.

"We're going to be okay," he told his little sister while trying to convince himself that it was true. "Let's get your toys out and play."

He reached into the toy box that he and Hannah had moved from the nursery into the great room and pulled out a stuffed unicorn. Lindsey must have left it. What if she was looking for it? Maybe he should call Hannah to let her know it was here. Or better still, maybe he should drop it off tomorrow on his way home from work.

"You're pitiful," he said to himself. He held the unicorn out for his sister to take and was surprised when Avery let go of the chair she had been holding on to and took a step toward him. He held his breath. Her little mouth was closed tight and her eyes were fixed on him as she took another step.

"You're doing it, baby girl."

Avery smiled at him, clapped her hands together then fell back on her diaper-padded bottom. Her lips quivered and her eyes filled with tears.

"It's okay. You are amazing." William reached out and took her into his arms. He was so lucky that he had been there for this. He sobered. Hannah should have been there with him. He looked down at Avery. "Is there any chance you're up for an encore?"

Someone knocked on her door and Hannah pushed her computer to the side. Ever since she and Lindsey had returned to their apartment, her neighbors had been stopping by to see them. She had been glad to catch up with each of them, but wasn't up to making small talk right now. She had felt empty ever since she and Lindsey had packed up their car at William's and headed home. It was if she had left some part of herself behind, and she was pretty sure that it was her heart.

"William?" she said before she stepped back so that he and Avery could enter. She immediately took Avery into her arms, she had missed the little girl so much.

"You won't believe what happened. She took two steps," William said, dropping the diaper bag on the living room floor.

"Really? She was so close before I left." And by leaving when she had, she had missed it.

"Watch." William took Avery out of her arms, stood her against the couch and then held out his hands to her. The toddler stared at him, dropped to the floor and crawled to the two of them.

Hannah started to laugh at the crestfallen look on his face. "She's not a trick puppy dog. She's going to walk when she's ready. Besides, she has a truckload of your Cooper stubbornness in her."

The joy left William's eyes and his voice turned somber. "Have you ever thought that there was something that you didn't like, but when you finally tried it, you found it wasn't so bad, after all? Maybe even more than that. Maybe you found out that you really couldn't live without it?"

"Like broccoli?" Hannah asked. She wasn't sure where this conversation was going, but she didn't care. Just having him to talk to was enough.

"Yeah, like broccoli. It looks all green and strange before you taste it, then you put some cheese sauce on it—because who doesn't like cheese sauce?—and you find out it's really quite good." William turned away from her then turned back around. "I'm not very good at all of this emotional stuff. I'm going to mess up."

Hannah held her breath. He was talking in terms of the future. "We all mess up, William. It's part of life."

"I've spent most of my life convincing myself that I didn't need anyone else in my life. I thought I was being strong taking on the world by myself. But now I know I was just too scared to take a chance on someone caring about me," William said.

For a moment, Hannah was confused. While he thought he was describing himself, he could have been describing her just, as well. She had left him because she had been too scared that he would turn away from her if she told him how she felt.

"When I told Maria that I didn't need anyone else, I was lying," he said as he moved closer and brushed his fingers down her face. "I do need you, Hannah. I need both you and Lindsey."

Hannah froze in place. She'd prepared herself to never feel his touch again and now he was offering her so much more. She had to make a decision. She could put herself out there with William and risk getting hurt. Or she could let fear keep her from what she wanted the most.

"I love—"

"No—" he sealed her lips with his before raising his head to look her in the eyes "—I want to say it first. I love you, Hannah. I love you with every beat of my heart."

"And that family you swore you'd never want? You seemed pretty adamant that family life wasn't for you," she said.

"What did I know? I'm just a simple brain surgeon who found out that, sometimes, if you're lucky, some unexpected miracle comes along that changes your whole life."

He brushed his lips against hers again. "That's what you are to me. You are my unexpected family."

EPILOGUE

HANNAH PUSHED THE side door from the garage open and placed the stack of books on the kitchen counter. The house was quiet and some of the excitement she had felt on her drive home disappeared. She'd known that William had planned to take Lindsey to her riding lesson with Sarah after work, but when she had called to tell him her good news, she'd hoped that he would cancel Lindsey's lesson so they all could celebrate together tonight.

Taking a bottle out of the refrigerator, she'd started to head upstairs to change when she heard a giggle she would recognize anywhere. It was coming from the door that led outside. Stepping through it, she was stunned to see the group of people gathered in their backyard.

"What are you doing?" Hannah asked as she rubbed the small, round bump of her abdomen and watched Avery chase Lindsey across the yard.

"We're having a celebration, of course," William said, turning the steaks he was cooking on the grill.

"You did all this for me?" she asked, stunned he'd pulled this together so quickly. It had only been this morning that she'd gotten the call that she had been accepted into Houston University's medical school program.

Suddenly, she was surrounded by her friends—some from work and others from her college classes—all wanting to congratulate her. She couldn't ever remember having a party planned just for her. Except for her wedding reception, of course.

"So, William tells me the plan is for you two to have a joint practice," Sarah said when the others had moved on to where William was passing out the steaks. "I'm not going to lie. It takes a lot to coordinate your work life with your family life when you're in the healthcare field, but I know you can do it."

"William's been very supportive. And Lindsey, too, of course. She can't wait to take care of a little brother. With those two behind me, I know it will all work out," Hannah told Sarah as they joined the others at the picnic table. As her friend went to join David, Hannah stopped to look across the backyard.

"What are you thinking?" William asked as he came up behind her and pulled her back against him.

"Just that I was right. This home was definitely meant for a family," she said, leaning into him and thinking about the man who had sworn he hadn't needed anyone in his life.

He had changed so much since that day.

They had both changed as they'd learned to trust each other, that depending on one another didn't make them weak. It made them stronger.

"No, this home wasn't meant for a family." William he rested his hands over their growing child. "It was meant for ours."

* * * * *